Love Don't Love Nobody

By:

Crusher & Dorian Sykes

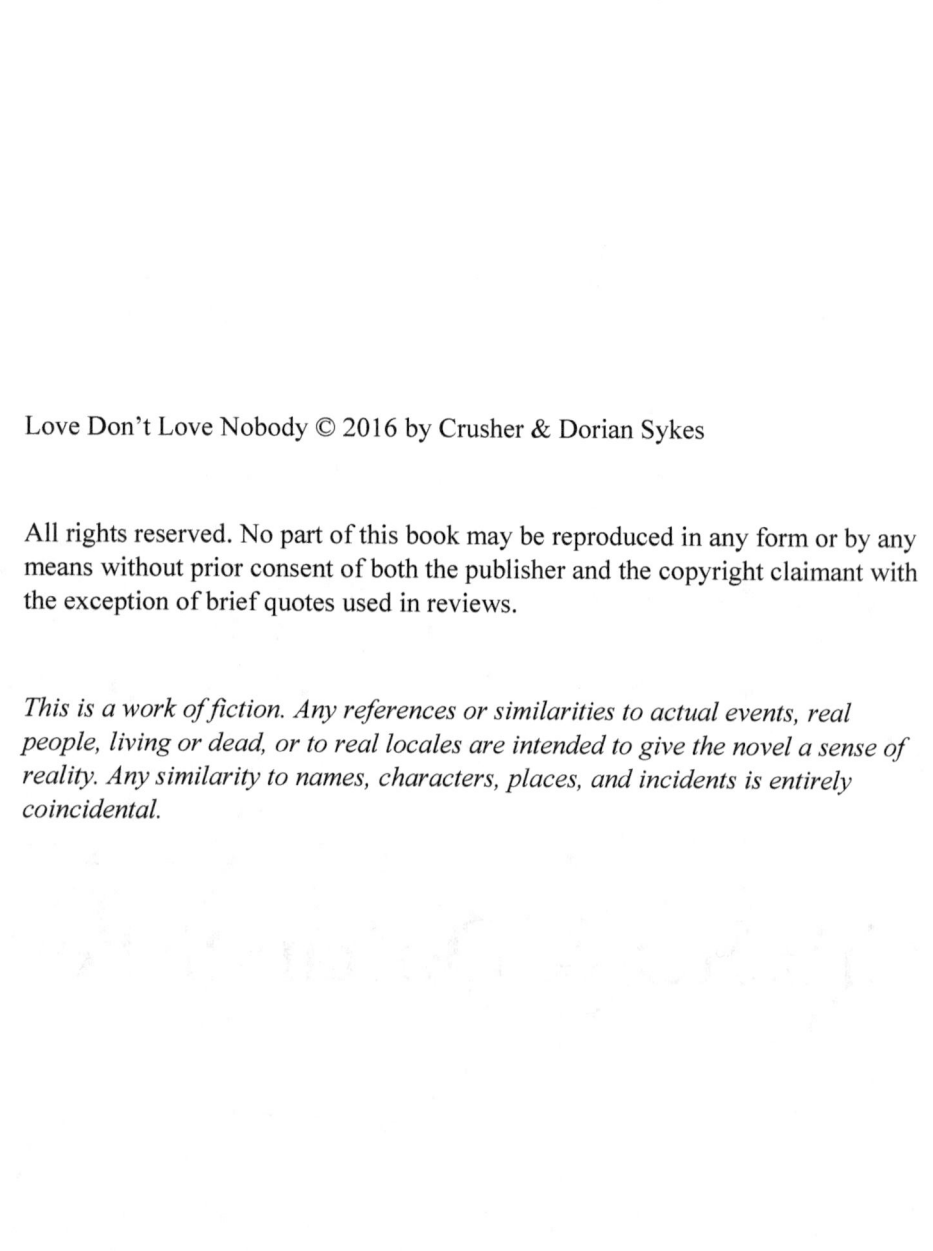

Love Don't Love Nobody © 2016 by Crusher & Dorian Sykes

Attn: Deborah Leff
 Pardon Attorney
 United States Department of Justice
 1425 New York Avenue, N.W. Suite 11000
 Washington, D.C. 20530 – 001

Re: Johnny Jackson
 Reg. No. 00220 – 748
 USP – Beaumont, Texas

Commutation of Sentence Petition of Johnny Jackson 00220 –748

Dear Deborah Leff:

On behalf of Johnny Jackson, and myself _____ (print name), as a citizen of the United States who supports the exercise of clemency (including pardon, commutation of sentence, remission of fine or restitution and reprieve, but not limited to other form). I humbly request that you grant Mr. Jackson's request for a commutation of sentence. It is my firm belief that Mr. Jackson deserves a second chance to atone for his past transgressions against the community at large.

Mr. Jackson was sentenced to 100 years imprisonment as a first time non-violent drug offender at the age of 22. It is true that Mr. Jackson made an unwise and imperceptible decision when he became involved with drugs as a young man growing up in Stateway Housing Projects. Mr. Jackson was young and naïve to believe that no other options or alternatives existed as a means to support his family (parents, sisters, and children), other than selling drugs. I acknowledge that he did, in fact, break the law and deserves to be punished; but a 100-year sentence is not a just punishment. This once unwise and naïve young man has spent over 16 years learning the error of his ways; and deserves the opportunity to redeem himself in the eyes of those who love and support him, as well as the community at large. While incarcerated, he has become an advocate for other inmates to obtain their General Education Diploma G. E. D., and if released, hopes to continue this type of volunteerism to prevent incarceration of at risk youth. It is my heartfelt belief that Mr. Jackson should certainly be a candidate selected for commutation of sentence.

I respectfully ask that you grant Mr. Jackson a commutation of sentence clemency. Thank you for your time and consideration of our expressed views.

Sincerely,

_____
Signature

_____
Address

_____
City, State & Zip Code

Attn: President Barack Obama
1600 Pennsylvania Ave. N.W.
Washington, D.C. 20500

Re: Johnny Jackson
Reg. No. 00220 – 748
USP – Beaumont, Texas

Commutation of Sentence Petition of Johnny Jackson 00220 –748

Dear Mr. President:

On behalf of Johnny Jackson, and myself _____ (print name), as a citizen of the United States who supports the exercise of clemency (including pardon, commutation of sentence, remission of fine or restitution and reprieve, but not limited to other form). I humbly request that you grant Mr. Jackson's request for a commutation of sentence. It is my firm belief that Mr. Jackson deserves a second chance to atone for his past transgressions against the community at large.

Mr. Jackson was sentenced to 100 years imprisonment as a first time non-violent drug offender at the age of 22. It is true that Mr. Jackson made an unwise and imperceptible decision when he became involved with drugs as a young man growing up in Stateway Housing Projects. Mr. Jackson was young and naïve to believe that no other options or alternatives existed as a means to support his family (parents, sisters, and children), other than selling drugs. I acknowledge that he did, in fact, break the law and deserves to be punished; but a 100-year sentence is not a just punishment. This once unwise and naïve young man has spent over 16 years learning the error of his ways; and deserves the opportunity to redeem himself in the eyes of those who love and support him, as well as the community at large. While incarcerated, he has become an advocate for other inmates to obtain their General Education Diploma G. E. D., and if released, hopes to continue this type of volunteerism to prevent incarceration of at risk youth. It is my heartfelt belief that Mr. Jackson should certainly be a candidate selected for commutation of sentence.

I respectfully ask that you grant Mr. Jackson a commutation of sentence clemency. Thank you for your time and consideration of our expressed views.

Sincerely,

_____
Signature

_____
Address

_____
City, State & Zip Code

~ Table of Contents ~

Acknowledgments

Dedication

Prologue

Chapter 1

Chapter 2

Chapter 3

Chapter 4

Chapter 5

Chapter 6

Chapter 7

Chapter 8

Chapter 9

Chapter 10

Chapter 11

Chapter 12

Chapter 13

Chapter 14

Chapter 15

Chapter 16

Chapter 17

Chapter 18

Chapter 19

Chapter 20

Chapter 21

Chapter 22

Chapter 23

Chapter 24

Chapter 25

˜ Acknowledgements ˜

To my beautiful mother, Ms. Leslie K. Sykes, I know this is your favorite book of mine, so I hope it makes you happy to finally see it on shelves.

Ms. Yolander Boston, you saw it in me from the start and you gave me my first publishing deal. That deal has opened up the door to many opportunities and has changed the course of my life. I thank you!

My crazy-ass homie from Chi-town, 'Sean G'. What's up, Charlie? You were with me back when it was all a dream. You laughed at me, but you never once doubted me.

My power agent, G. Branch. I appreciate all your hard work and honesty. Good people are truly hard to come by.

'B. Gizzle'! What's up, Round? It's 'bout dat time to rock up this here Guilty by Association demonstration, ya dig? Holla at me.

To all my readers who've been rocking with me from the start…much love for all of your support. I'm going to keep 'em coming at y'all for as long as y'all will have me.

D. Skyes

~ Dedication~

This novel is dedicated to my beloved grandmother, Ms. Carolyn A. Sykes, who inspired the title of this book. Grams, you shol' know what to say.

~ Prologue ~

Henry's Palace has always been a haven for well-to-do housewives, hustler's wives, and elite business-women, seeking a night of pleasure away from their mundane home lives. Since the 80's women have been sneaking out with their girlfriends for ladies night out, most carrying on affairs with the lustful eye-candy stripping at the club. Henry's Palace is the male version of King of Diamonds. Their motto is, "At Henry's every fantasy can be fulfilled."

"Work that mothafucka! Work that mothafucka!" Marie demanded as she stood at the foot of the stage making it rain with tens and twenties. She was nearly in a trance of infatuation as she showered the stripper working the stage.

"Spend that money, Gurl!" shouted Nicky.

Skyy and Nicky laughed and egged Marie on. Since they first introduced her to the quiet secret society of women, she had really come out of her shell.

The dancer's set ended and the DJ took an intermission.

"That nigga got a third leg," Marie said, taking her seat.

They all high-fived and laughed in agreement. They had a reserved booth perched for prime center action. Nicky and Skyy were on the club's V.I.P. list and were treated nothing shy of royalty whenever they patronized the spot because they were known for spending big money. Their booth would always greet them with buckets of champagne and no less the two grand in singles depending on what type of night it was. Tonight was the typical ladies' night out. Dick and chiseled abs were wall-to-wall and the women were spending money like it was going out of style.

Skyy excused herself away from the table and went to the ladies' room. On her way back she noticed Chris sitting with another woman near the back of the club. He ain't on business, Skyy thought, taking a quick inventory of the ambiance. He wasn't giving her a lap dance or trying to work her out of a dollar. No, instead he was extra close and was obviously flirting with the woman. The bitch was busted according to Skyy's appraisal. He could have at least been fucking with a dime.

Chris didn't even notice Skyy now standing over him. He was too busy cooing in ole' girl's ear.

"Chris!" Skyy yelled and then smacked her lips as if to say, "Really?"

Chris sat up a notch, but he didn't quite acknowledge Skyy how she expected him to.

"I didn't know you was comin' through tonight," he said.

"I can see that," Skyy replied, rolling her eyes over towards ole' girl.

"Chris, I didn't know you were married," the woman said in a tone that let Sky know that her statement was a lug meant for her.

"What, Bitch? You tryna get cute?" Skyy snapped.

"Hold up! Who you callin' a bitch, Bitch?"

The woman went to stand up, but Skyy grabbed a half-full Moet bottle and slapped the woman across the side of her face with it. Chris disappeared into the shadows while Skyy straddled the woman on the sectional sofa and proceeded to beat the hell out of her.

"Girl, look!" Marie said, pointing towards the back of the club. "Ain't that Skyy back there?"

Nicky kicked off his shoes under the table. "Sho' is." He ran to assist Skyy. "Here, let me get the bitch!" Nicky pulled Skyy off of the woman.

Marie and Erica also ran to Skyy's aid. They took turns rag-dogging the woman until the bouncers came and broke it up. They were tossed out of the door and into the parking lot where they laughed it up, staggering in the direction of their cars. It was common for this sort of thing to happen on any given night. Damn near every night there would be some type of drama. It was to be expected at Henry's Palace.

~ Chapter 1 ~

"Love don't live here...love don't live here anymore," Skyy sang while doing her morning exercise. She was grooving to Faith Evans. It was now her theme song. Every morning she woke up at the crack of dawn and got her Jane Fonda on.

"Finished," she said, out of breath. She'd just completed her last set of squats and they were indeed serving their purpose. Skyy was in perfect shape. She stood 5'7 and was 140 pounds of all ass and titties. Skyy was what niggas referred to as a 'red bone'. Her hair was silky black and fell down damn near to her behind. She was the total package.

Skyy stood in front of her workout mirror looking at her calves and rear-end. Satisfied that everything was at its best, she grabbed an awaiting towel and headed towards the bathroom. She showered while still listening to Faith considering that the album was on repeat. After showering, she walked over to one of the two walk-in closets located in the master bedroom which was one of five rooms within her colonial home. Her house was located five minutes outside of Detroit in Gross Pointe. It was a bit of a suburb—you had to have a few dollars to live out there. The house was equipped with an in-ground swimming pool, an attached guesthouse, and a three-car garage. Skyy and Matt, also known as E-Way, had purchased the home six months earlier after E-Way settled out of court for two million dollars regarding a civil suit.

One night while at a gas station, E-Way was approached from behind by two men who were both wearing hooded sweat shirts and brandishing guns. One of the men put his pistol to E-Way's head and told him not to make a scene. He forced E-Way to get in the back seat of his car.

Realizing that the men wanted something more than just money and that they were attempting to kidnap him, E-Way pushed the man back giving himself enough time to run. The two gunmen fired several rounds at him as he ran for his life. He managed to fire back a few rounds while scrambling to safety. The Arab working at the gas station locked the doors of the convenience store leaving E-Way to fend for himself.

The two men finally retreated as a Detroit police car pulled onto the scene. Without warning, the two white officers fired several rounds at E-Way as he stood at the door of the gas station with his gun still in hand. He was hit eight times and was placed in ICU. E-Way remained in the hospital for two months recovering from his wounds while Skyy hired an attorney to file the suit against the Detroit Police Department claiming negligence and pain and suffering.

Skyy and E-Way had been boyfriend and girlfriend for five years, kicking it since the eleventh grade. E-Way was your average dope boy prior to getting the settlement. He was getting a little money, but once he received the settlement check he began to live out his 'Maserati Rick' fantasies. He purchased their home, three late model cars, jewelry for himself and Skyy, and enough dope to supply half of Detroit. He also gave Skyy some money to open up a salon. For the most part E-Way was good people, not to mention that he was an attractive brother. He stood at six feet and three inches and was about 210 pounds. He was dark-skinned, bald, had perfect white teeth, and swagger like no other.

Skyy browsed through the many shoes and clothes inside of her closet. She selected a Dolce and Gabbana outfit that she'd recently bought along with a pair of white stilettos to match. It was a shorts set, white with red piping, and it fit Skyy like a glove. She grabbed one of her Gucci handbags and walked over to her jewelry box. She decided to rock a pair of five-carat diamond stud earrings, a matching tennis bracelet, her white gold necklace, and a mother-of-pearl Rolex watch. She modeled in front of the mirror inspecting every aspect of her ensemble. Satisfied with her achieved level of pretty, Skyy walked into the bedroom and kissed E-Way goodbye. He was sound asleep after running the streets the night before.

She was off to the salon. Skyy dropped the top on her 645 BMW and enjoyed the morning sun as she drove down Houston Whittier. It was summer time and that was exactly what was bumping from Skyy's sound system—Will Smith's "Summer Time". She pulled into her parking spot at the shop and made her entrance. She was greeted with the usual phony "Hey, how you doing" from the assorted hating ass, low-budget bitches who were either getting their hair done or doing hair, with the exception of Nicky.

"Where you going, Ms. Thang? To an audition of Luke's new video?" Nicky asked as he examined Skyy from head to toe.

"You got jokes, huh?" Skyy laughed, not at all offended because she knew that Nicky was only playing.

Nicky's real name was Nicholas. He was a homosexual, but let him tell it he was a woman trapped in a man's body. Skyy and Nicky were best friends and had been since third grade. As far back as Skyy could remember Nicky had always been gay. Even as a child he was a bit different. He may have been gay, but he had always been a real mothafucka, which was why he and Skyy became best friends. Both Nicky and Skyy grew up poverty-stricken. Skyy was raised by her late grandmother who had passed away when Skyy was sixteen. Life had always been rough for Skyy. Coming up, her grandmother would take her to the Salvation Army thrift store to buy hand-me-downs for school clothes. Skyy's mother, Trina, was a crack head. Her father, James, turned her mother out to the streets at the age of fifteen. As a result, they both became full-blown addicts. Skyy would only see them when she was walking to and from school. They'd be at the corner-store panhandling and Trina would often be trying to turn a trick.

By the fifth grade, Nicky began stealing from the local malls, trying to keep up with the Joneses. He tried turning Skyy out to stealing but she wasn't good at it so Nicky, being the friend that he was, kept Skyy laced with all of the latest fads. Whatever Nicky stole for himself he made sure that Skyy had it too. If it wasn't for Nicky, Skyy probably wouldn't have graduated because she hated going to school in the clothes that her grandmother bought her. When her grandmother passed away, Skyy had nowhere to live. Her grandmother didn't have any life insurance, which left Skyy broke and homeless. All of her relatives had kids and problems of their own, so to live with one of her aunts meant to endure even worse conditions than while living with her grandmother. It was Nicky who copped an apartment along with a Nissan Maxima for the two of them to share. Nicky turned his petty shoplifting into a hustle and started boosting. The boy was so cold that he'd take orders from customers before going to the mall. Nicky's boosting paid for prom, senior trips, and everything in between. Skyy felt like she owed Nicky her life, so when E-Way received his settlement she vowed to open a salon simply because Nicky had always wanted his own shop. He and Skyy were now partners.

"Girl, you know I'm just being silly," Nicky said as he stood twirling a pair of curlers while finishing up one of his early morning clients. "Turn around and let me see the whole set."

It was Thursday and every chicken-head with a balla for a boyfriend / sponsor was getting ready for the weekend. By Sunday they'd be in need of a fresh do.

Alina, one of the shop's hairstylists, said something smart under her breath as Skyy modeled her new fit for Nicky and of course the haters.

"You likes?" Skyy asked, striking a pose.

"You stay killin' shit. That's why you my girl, I'm a have to go snatch me one of them shits. I know Devin wouldn't mind seeing all this in one of those," Nicky said, rubbing his girlish frame.

Everyone in the shop burst out laughing at the thought of Nicky in a tight fitting outfit. Nicky was hella funny. He was the life of the shop. He stood at five feet, eight inches and was 165 pounds. He had a caramel complexion, hazel contacts, and whore his hair in short perm brushed waves. Nicky was one of those dudes that you look at and at first sight you just knew he was gay. Everything about him from his wiggly walk to his clothes said, "I'm gay."

Skyy laughed right along with the crowd. "I'm sure he wouldn't."

Devin was Nicky's current boyfriend—another one of those down-low, 'I'm not gay' ass niggas. Who did they think they were fooling?

As usual, the shop was jam packed. It was that way on any given day from morning until closing, which was sometimes after ten o'clock depending on how much a bitch was spending. The shop was called Elite. Skyy and Nicky chose the name in an effort to eliminate the riff-raff, and separate the ballas from the fakers. That way they could charge top-notch prices. As a business major and ghetto entrepreneur, Skyy knew how to appease the urban economy. Blacks tend to go for the most expensive shit they can find just to be able to say, "I paid X amount of dollars for this here." Skyy suffered from the same insecurities that many other young blacks did. She had to have the best of everything.

The shop's name was fitting—everyone inside of the salon indeed felt they were elite, from the customers to its owners. The shop was located on the eastside of Detroit on 7 Mile and Mackay. It was the old Secretary of State building which had been closed down because it kept getting robbed. It consisted of five booths which housed four hair stylists and one barber. There was also a station near the entrance for a nail technician. The shop was very spacious and comfortable. In the waiting area sat two black leather sectional couches, two love seats, and a few recliners. All of the latest magazines filled the two coffee tables and there was a stack of DVDS for the 42-inch Plasma mounted on the wall. The floor was white granite giving the illusion of marble. Everything about the shop was elite.

Nicky manned the first booth. Next to him was Alina, a bad ass mixed broad from the Buffalo Projects. She and Skyy were neck and neck as far as looks, but for some reason they couldn't stand each other. They kept it professional though and remained cool on the strength of Nicky. Alina and Nicky became friends while attending cosmetology school together. On the other side of Alina station was Marie. She was a petite, dark-skinned sista from Oak Park, Michigan. She grew up in the suburbs but had also gone to school with Nicky and Alina. Marie was quiet. She was always watching and soaking up game from the many game-running hoes at the shop. Nicky would always tease her saying she was as square as a pool table and twice as green. Marie earned her booth because she brought the suburban clientele to the shop, plus she was very creative. She created several new hairstyles that earned the shop spots in local hair magazines and hair shows.

Next to Marie was Tae, the old head of the shop. Tae was in her late sixties but looked no part of it. She had been doing hair since Diana Ross was with the Supremes. Tae was hella jazzy. She wore her hair cut short and stood at a mere five feet, four inches with a petite frame that was still intact. Tae was good people and was very knowledgeable of the industry. Skyy and Nicky rented Tae her booth because she was good for the money and she brought the older clientele to the shop.

Joe was the shop's barber. He was the only man who worked in the shop. A young brother from the Westside, Joe was quiet, brown-skinned with a medium build, about five feet, nine inches, and 180 pounds. Joe landed his position at Elite for reason not related to his craft. He too was a down-low brotha. He had met Nicky at a gay bar and learned that Nicky was part owner of the salon. To earn his position, he had to pay like he weighed—fucking and sucking Nicky.

Across from Joe was Erica, the nail tech. The girl was always late but she was tolerated because she was always on time with her booth rent. Plus, she kept everyone laughing. She'd cuss you out in a minute while smiling and if your gear wasn't up to par you best believe that Erica was going to pull you up. She was one of the few real ones. She always spoke her mind no matter whose feelings were at stake. Erica was what niggas call 'funny built'. She was all chest and no ass. She kept her attire on one thousand though as well as her hair and nails. She was five feet, six inches, 175 pounds, dark brown, and wore wire-framed Cartier glasses.

Skyy's nook was in the back room. She didn't do hair, but she'd go to the shop every morning just to have something to do.

"So what's the deal, Skyy?" Nicky asked. He'd just finished up his customer's hair and was waiting on the new shampoo girl, Veronica, to finish with his next head.

"Ain't much. Looking forward to tonight. We're still on aren't we?" Skyy asked.

Once a week, sometimes twice, the salon would have ladies night out at the local male strip club, Henry's Palace.

"Babe, I'm going to have to pass," Nicky told Skyy. "I already got some ass lined up. Devin is taking me over to Canada tonight."

"Sounds romantic," Skyy said, a bit disappointed.

"I guess it would be ro-*man*-tic considering," Erica said with a laugh.

Everyone caught the sly statement and began laughing. She was trying to be funny since Nicky and Devin were both men. Everyone was laughing with the exception of Nicky. He was a little salty so he shifted the spotlight.

"I know your undercover brotha ass ain't over there snickering and what not!" Nicky snapped, looking directly at Joe.

Everyone ceased in their laughter and waited for Joe to reply to Nicky's bold allegations. No one knew about Nicky and Joe's fling except Skyy and she too was all ears waiting for Joe to respond.

"That's what I thought, Snack Butt," Nicky said. "I knew you ain't have shit to say for real."

Joe had the shit face. He continued to cut the gentleman's hair that was seated in his chair, pretending not to hear Nicky. But, Erica wasn't letting it go that easy.

"Say it ain't so, Joe," Erica said then burst out laughing. "I knew you had a lil' sugar in yo' tank. Ya' damn near pretty as me," she continued in between laughs. She was riding Joe's ass like a professional comic. She couldn't even finish the young lady's nails because she was laughing so hard that she was in tears.

"Alright, alright, Erica. That's enough," Skyy chimed in. "Y'all know Joe isn't gay. Isn't that right, Nicky?" she asked in an attempt to clean up the mess. She was looking at it from a business standpoint. She didn't want Joe to feel uncomfortable and quit. "Isn't that right, Nicky?" she repeated herself.

Reluctantly, Nicky retracted his statement. "That's right. Joe's not gay. Although he does act like it sometimes."

"Uh-huh," Erica said. "Don't try to clean that shit up now."

"Girl, you know you's a mess." Tae laughed.

It was just another day at the shop—gossip on top of more gossip.

"Aight, my man. Good looking out," said the man whose hair Joe was cutting. He examined his fresh cut. "What I owe you?" he asked, standing to his feet and handing Joe back the mirror."

"Fifteen dollars," Joe answered.

All of the women in the salon were gawking at the six foot, one inch, 200-pound light-brown-skinned, well-groomed brother.

"Damn he's fine," one woman said as she looked over the Essence magazine she was reading. Marie was doing her hair.

"Uh-huh, Girl," Marie whispered.

Skyy was checking out the man's behind as he stood with his back to her. After paying Joe, the man looked in the mirror one last time and was about to turn and leave, but he noticed Skyy staring at him. She immediately broke the glance and reached for a magazine on the coffee table from her seated position on one of the recliners. The guy smiled and turned to face Joe.

"A look, my name's Mario, Man, and I was hoping you could cut my hair on the regular," he said. "No one has ever been able to get my line as straight as you got it."

"Any time, Man. Just stop thru. Here's my card. I even do appointments, "Joe advised.

"Aight. Good looking." Mario took the card and then headed for the door. "Y'all ladies have a nice day," he said, looking at Skyy in particular.

"Girl, did you see how that nigga was eyeing Skyy?" Nicky asked after the door closed.

"I thought the nigga was looking at me for real, for real," Alina said in a matter-of-fact tone of voice.

"And I always thought you were a bit cross-eyed," Skyy remarked.

"Ooohh weeee," Erica said, instigating as always.

"But anyhow, you hoes know what time of the week it is. See me before ya' leave and please have my cheese," Skyy said. With that, she went off to her office. She sat at her Dell computer surfing the internet, looking at handbags and shoes while eating her favorite cheat food, soft batch chocolate chip cookies.

Chapter 2

Meanwhile, E-Way made his way to his hood. He hated being at home. The only time he went home was at night to go to sleep. No sooner than Skyy left for the shop he was up and at 'em. E-Way owned a bar on Mt. Elliot called Tippin' End. He bought it from Old Man Frank out of his settlement money. E-Way grew up in a historical mansion four houses down from the bar. He used to run numbers for Old Frank as a youngin' and when Frank decided to retire from the streets E-Way made him a proposition for the bar. Old Man Frank not only sold E-Way the bar, but he also gave him his connect. Old Man Frank had been dealing dope since the 70's and had never been caught. He was now in his mid 70's and felt it was time to pass the torch.

Every morning E-Way and his street team who called themselves 'KFB' (Known for Balling) would all meet up at the bar and break bread. KFB was a neighborhood click that E-Way and his best friend Bubbles started back in high school. Its members consisted of Kev, Chuck, Chuckie Boms, Big Whitney, Bubbles, and E-Way. Together they were really known for balling. Everything was boss this, boss that. That's what they called themselves individually. They'd tell you in a minute, "I'm a boss, Bitch. Boss up!" That was their motto.

E-Way had invested in some studio equipment which he put in the upstairs of the bar. He formed a record label called Floss-A-Lot using the members of KFB as artists. They put out several independent projects and soon became local celebrities. They had the entire city saying, "Boss up!" As with anything else, the haters and competitors came out mimicking. In this case the haters were known as Murkland Niggas. They were from the flip side of 7 Mile. They were in the same age bracket as E-Way and his boys, They'd all gone to Pershing High School and had been feuding ever since then.

E-Way parked his Range Rover behind the assorted European whips that lined the front of the bar. He entered the ground floor of the establishment, which was empty, and walked upstairs to the studio to find Kev, Chuck, and Bubbles smoking blunts and recording their new song "What Cha' Is".

Chuck was the youngest one of the bunch but he was getting just as much money. He stood five feet, six inches and was 150 pounds. He was shit black, wore a bald fade, and stayed fresh to death. He was in the sound booth getting ready to record the chorus and was in mode, tipping his Cartier Buffalo frames and swinging his Floss-A-Lot chain from side to side. The whole click had chains just like it.

"You ready?" asked Bubbles, who was working the switchboard.

"Yeah, Man," Chuck replied. "Real niggas don't count money. Bitch, we weigh it. Got work for the low, got K's for haters. Pull up, jump out stuntin'. Bitch, you know who I is. I'm a boss fo' sho'. I'm 'bout my dough," Chuck recited, dropping the chorus.

E-Way, Bubbles, and Kev were all bobbing to the beat as it played back.

"That shit nice," E-Way said as he rolled his first blunt of the day.

Big Whitney, Chuckie Boms, and a little busto broad all entered the studio.

"Who this?" asked Bubbles, referring to the young lady.

"Oh, she on the house. You want some head, Nigga?" Big Whitney asked. He was in boss mode.

"Hell yeah!" Bubbles answered, taking the young lady into the back room.

"I got next!" hollered E-Way. "Aight, now that everybody's here let's get to it. What you do last night, Kev?" E-Way asked. He was asking how much money Kev's houses made.

Chuck and Chuckie Boms gave E-Way a duffle bag with close to fifty grand in it.

"Aight, I'm 'bout to re-up. I should be straight this afternoon. Y'all can pick the shit up then," E-Way advised.

When he'd gotten his lawsuit, E-Way bought twenty kilos using the connect that Old Man Frank plugged him with. E-Way gave Big Whitney, Kev, Bubbles, Chuck, and Chuckie Boms each two bricks. He did that just on the strength so that everyone could get their money right. The deal was that they would cop from E-Way and he would give them the work for the low-low.

"Y'all niggas ready for the show tomorrow?" E-Way asked.

Their record label was sponsoring a concert at the State Theatre. They had B.G. from the Hot Boys as the headliner while they would be the opening act.

"Man, we gon' ball out, Baby! We gots to do this new track right here," Kev insisted.

Kev, Chuckie Boms, and Big Whitney were the stars of the label. Bubbles, Chuck, and E-Way were more like features. E-Way couldn't rap a lick, but he would be on skits talking cash shit. They didn't expect to make it big time; they just wanted to be hood stars.

"Damn, Dogg! What, you back there making love to the bitch?" snapped Chuck, looking at his watch.

Chuck and Chuckie Boms were best friends. They could even pass for brothers. They both had dark-brown skin, were about six feet even, and were of medium build. Big Whitney was every bit of 350 pounds. He was six foot, two inches, light-skinned, and had no neck. When he breathed he always sounded as if he was out of breath. Bubbles was about six foot, one inch, dark-skinned, with short, nappy hair, and bags under his eyes. He always looked tired.

"Was the head right?" E-Way asked, talking to Bubbles who'd just entered the room sweating.

"One thousand," Bubbles answered.

The crew continued to work on their songs, smoke weed, and talk boss shit. That was their daily routine: meet up at the bar, chill, and run trains on bustos.

***

It was nine o'clock and Skyy had been at the shop all day making sure that everyone paid their booth rent before leaving. She wasn't in a rush to leave because E-Way was never home and Nicky had canceled their ladies night out ritual. Skyy was still in the back room surfing the internet when Marie came in to grab her purse.

"Girl, it's after nine. What are you still doing here?" Marie asked. "I know you're hitting Henry's tonight."

"Nicky canceled on me. She has a date with Devin," Skyy said with as much sarcasm as she could.

"Shit, Girl, Nicky's ass don't make no party. You and I can go. Plus, I think Tae and Erica are supposed to be going too. Come on. It'll be fun."

"Let me finish up. Give me about ten minutes and I'll be ready," Skyy agreed. She waited for Marie to go back out front and then called E-Way's cell phone. "Hey, Baby. Where are you?" she asked when he answered.

"At the studio. I'm about to open the bar in a minute."

"What time are you coming home?"

"Don't wait up."

"When are we going to spend some time together, Baby?"

"You know I'm trying to recoup some of this money. Look at all the shit we done bought. You know I'm on the grind, Ma."

Skyy couldn't complain because E-Way was putting out a lot of money and he had been more than good to her.

"I promise we'll spend some time together this weekend."

"Okay, but be safe, Baby. And call me when you're on your way home," Skyy said, ending the conversation. She shut down her computer, rose from her seat, and entered the front of the salon. "You ready?"

"Where y'all going?" Nicky asked.

"Marie and I are going to Henry's."

"I want details, you hear me? Details!" Nicky demanded as he finished up his last head.

Skyy and Marie took Skyy's car because they wanted to pull up in style. They had the top dropped trying to enjoy the warm summer night. Skyy pulled into the parking lot of Henry's Palace to valet her car. They were eyed by the many women as they were escorted to the V.I.P. seats on center stage. Skyy and Nicky were regulars at Henry's Palace. Marie had just started going, but she had become a regular as of lately. They ordered a bottle of Moet and waited for the festivities to begin.

"I heard Mr. Marcus is supposed to be here tonight," Skyy stated as she looked around the club spotting Tae and Erica.

"That nigga got a horse dick, Girl." Marie laughed.

"His ass looks like a horse too," added Skyy, "but he sho' know how to work that mothafucka."

"Amen, Girl. You see how he be punishing them hoes in those pornos? He could beat this pussy up any time he wants to," Marie admitted, taking a sip of bubbly.

"I can't wait 'til my baby comes out," Skyy said.

"Who?"

"Chris' sexy ass." Skyy's head was swiveling, hoping that she spotted him.

"That nigga is that deal. I bet he can fuck his ass off."

"Oh can he!" Skyy leaned her head back thinking about their last episode.

"You and Chris? Oh my God! Girl, when?"

"Three days ago," Skyy admitted with a grin of pleasure.

"How long y'all been kicking it?"

"For a few months."

"You better be careful. You know E-Way's ass is crazy."

"Yeah, I know. But I got this."

Chris was Skyy's 'thang-thang' as she referred to him. She was getting from him what E-Way wasn't giving her—good dick. In return, Skyy took extra care of Chris, spending E-Way's money while doing it.

"Ahhhhh!" Every woman in the club screamed as the lights dimmed and the show began. Four cock strong brothas hit the stage wearing nothing but a pair of tight Speedos. They were gleaming from the lights and the baby oil which covered their bodies.

"Work that mothafucka! Work that mothafucka!" the women chanted. Those were the lyrics to the song that was playing.

Skyy was bouncing to the beat and sipping her Moet while enjoying an eye full. Marie was standing up throwing fists full of dollar bills onto the stage. One of the men jumped down and pushed Marie into her seat. He began bumping and grinding up against her, giving Marie an exclusive lap dance. He spun around and shook it up while Marie filled his drawers with bills. She was going crazy.

"Hand me my purse, Girl," Marie told Skyy. She promptly reached for more bills. "Work that mothafucka," she said, slapping the guy on his ass to the beat.

The club was going crazy just as any other night. Chris appeared on stage wearing his white thong Speedo and a cowboy hat. He was six foot, five inches, weighed 225 pounds (all muscle), was light-skinned, and had green eyes and deep-brushed waves. The nigga was a stallion. Women rushed the stage launching money to Chris' feet while he put on a show. Skyy, for the second time, felt a tinge of jealousy. She had to check her feelings. Chris finished his set and made his way over to Skyy and Marie's table.

"I see your fan club is in the building," Skyy said.

"Here you go. They was only enjoying the show. I know you enjoyed it," Chris replied, grabbing Skyy's hand and rubbing his twenty-pack with it.

Skyy smiled and started to feel better. She could feel Chris' fan club watching.

"How 'bout I put on a private show for you after the club? You'd like that?" Chris asked her.

"It's a date," Skyy answered.

Chris kissed her hand and then she excused herself.

"That nigga got game," Marie said rhythmically.

The ladies continued to enjoy themselves, ordering more Moet and watching the many fine brothas do their thing. Mr. Marcus, the main event, had the club going crazy. He came out wearing leopard print Speedos and the boy had a third leg. The women rushed him so hard that he had to remain on stage or risk the chance of being hurt. Marie had spent over five hundred dollars in the short time that they were there. She had indeed become a fanatic. She wanted to stay until closing, but Skyy was eager to leave so that she could hook up with Chris. So, Skyy dropped Marie back off at the shop to get her car.

"Aight, Girl. See you in the morning," Marie said, closing Skyy's door. "I want details!"

Skyy laughed at Marie as the woman staggered over to her car.

Chris lived downtown on Woodward in some recently constructed condos. Skyy raced on the Davidson expressway and looked at her watch. It was almost midnight. She wanted to hurry up and fuck Chris so that she could beat E-Way home. She had E-Way's schedule down to a science. She knew he wouldn't be home until at least three o'clock in the morning.

Chris answered the door wearing a similar pair of Speedos that he'd worn at the club and a silk robe which exposed his fine physique. At the sight of his abs Skyy became moist.

"Are you going to just stand there or are you going to come in?" Chris asked, breaking Skyy from her zone.

"Huh? Oh…yeah," she said, smiling before giving Chris a passionate kiss.

He shut the door while still holding Skyy. It was all business—no words were exchanged and the only sounds were their moans. Skyy removed Chris' robe and began kissing him all over, starting with his chest and then stopping at his Johnson. She helped him out of his Speedos and began jacking his dick.

"Suck it," Chris said in a soft, seductive yet demanding tone.

Skyy was turned on by Chris' authoritativeness. She did as she was told, taking Chris into her mouth and sucking him to death.

Chris pulled Skyy up from her knees and then walked her over to the sofa. He undressed her before laying her across the couch. He took her legs and wrapped them around his neck, mouthing her entire pussy. Skyy sighed with satisfaction while gripping and guiding Chris' head. Chris expertly ate Skyy up until she couldn't take it anymore and wanted to feel him inside of her. She pulled him up for air. She herself was breathing hard and was beginning to sweat.

"Fuck me," she told him.

Chris pinned Skyy's legs to her shoulders and began punishing the pussy. He was deep stroking her while she clawed his back.

"Ahhh. Oh! Fuck me! Fuck me!" Skyy screamed.

Chris turned her over, long stroking her from the back as she turned around to look into his eyes. Her soft yellow ass bounced against Chris' pelvis with every stroke. He was putting in work. Chris sat back, pulling Skyy onto his dick. He cuffed both ass cheeks and slid her up and down until he reached his climax. Skyy continued to ride Chris until he went completely limp. She kept him inside of her while kissing on his neck and ears in an attempt to get him back up. They went for round two and three. Skyy gave Chris the nick name 'Sweat' because he was known to sweat a bitch's perm out.

It was almost two o'clock and E-Way had yet to call Skyy. She wanted to continue to lay up but she couldn't chance it. If E-Way was to beat her home all hell would break loose.

"I have to get ready to get out of here," Skyy said as she laid spread eagle on the floor beside Chris.

"You can spend the night," he told her.

"You know I can't do that."

"And why is that?"

"Because I can't." She reached for her clothes. "I'll see you next week," she advised once fully dressed.

"You think you can wait that long?" Chris teased her as he stood at the front door to let her out.

"I doubt it, but it'll be worth the wait."

Chris kissed Skyy on the forehead and watched her walk to her car.

Skyy raced home feeling like a new woman. Chris had knocked the lining out of her ass. Her pussy was still pulsating. She pulled into the circular driveway of her house and was glad to see that she'd beaten E-Way home. She raced inside, stripped her clothes at the door, and then rushed to the bathroom. She took a quick shower, wrapped up her hair, and then was off to bed.

~ Chapter 3 ~

It was eight o'clock in the morning. Skyy woke up to find E-Way curled up next to her as always. She smiled at the thought of her and Chris' episode the night before. She and E-Way hadn't had sex in almost two weeks. Things had become monotonous. With E-Way it was like 'okay give me some head, bend over let me fuck you from the back'. Then he'd bust his nut and roll over. Still, they endured the adversity on the strength of their history.

Skyy got up and washed her face then headed down to the basement for her morning workout. She ran through her sets still thinking about Chris' sexy ass. She carried her thoughts into the shower which led to her getting off an early morning nut. She picked out her outfit for the day, got dressed, and was out of the door. On her way to the shop, she stopped at Burger King to grab some breakfast. While she was waiting on her order, Mario, the guy from the shop, entered the restaurant. He as with a little girl who appeared to be his daughter. Skyy noticed him first, but avoided eye contact because she didn't want him to think that she was staring.

The little girl pointed up at the menu telling her dad what she wanted. Mario placed their order and then stepped aside to wait for the food. He recognized Skyy as she stepped up to the counter to get her order. He wanted to say something but thought it'd be inappropriate since his daughter was with him.

Skyy turned to leave. As she passed him she flirtatiously let out, "You have a nice day."

"You too," Mario replied with a smile, enjoying the sight of Skyy's backside as she walked out.

"Who is that, Daddy?" Skyy could hear the little girl ask.

Skyy pulled in front of the salon and parked. It was another beautiful summer day. She was wearing a scarf over her head from the night before. As soon as she hit the door, she was escorted to the back room by Nicky.

"Excuse me," Nicky said to the woman whose hair he was doing. "I'll be right back."

Marie, not wanting to miss the details, also excused herself. No sooner than the door was closed, Nicky began drilling Skyy.

"Dish, Bitch," he told her. "I want full details."

Marie had pulled up a seat and was leaning on her hands in anticipation. "Well, how was it?" she asked impatiently.

Skyy flopped down in her desk chair and began recalling and almost reliving the night's events with Chris. "That nigga fucked me for almost two hours. I woke up and was still thinking about him. I couldn't even concentrate on my workout."

"Did he eat it?" Marie asked.

"Did he!" Skyy sighed. "It's like the first time every time."

"Don't let that nigga get your nose too far open," Nicky warned.

"I got this. He's just my lil thang-thang."

"Aight now. I'm telling you...don't go falling in love." Nicky looked at her knowingly.

With that, they all filed back out to the front. All eyes were on them as they re-entered the main room.

"Who you got next, Nicky?" Skyy asked. "I need you to touch me up."

"If Connie's big mouth ain't in here by the time I'm done, I'll get you next," Nicky answered.

Erica came dragging her tail through the door late as usual. She was wearing a pair of tinted Versace sunglasses instead of her usual wire frames. She had a hangover from the night before.

"Erica, you're late," Skyy said.

"Aren't I always?" Erica retorted. "But the important thing is that I'm here now. Chop, chop! Let's get to work shall we!" Erica laughed, trying to get Skyy to laugh along. "Ahhh. Lighten' up, Boss Lady," she stated sarcastically. "You know what your problem is?" She continued without waiting for Skyy to respond. "You're always here and don't have a job." Erica laughed some more.

"Girl, you crazy. Do my nails while I wait for Nicky to finish up."

"Is E-Way and them still performing today at the State Theatre?" Tae asked. She was in her sixties but was hip to the new era. She stayed laced in all the latest designers and hung out with people half her age.

"Yeah. I believe they hit the stage at nine," Skyy answered. "Y'all gon' fall through?"

"I don't fuck with local niggas," Alina replied.

"That's funny. Could you remind me who it is that you fuck with? Cause I mean…I ain't never seen no nigga up here for you," Skyy snapped.

Every time Alina tried to pop slick Skyy cut her ass up and put her back in her place.

"Ooohh weeee," Erica said, instigating as usual.

Skyy got her hair and nails done and then hung around the shop until the concert was set to start.

***

E-Way and the rest of Floss-A-Lot records were all backstage doing mic checks and trying to get ready for the show. E-Way peeked out into the crowd from behind curtain and didn't see one empty seat. Kev, Chuck, Chuckie Boms, Bubbles, and Big Whitney were smoking L's, standing in a circle passing blunt after blunt. They had four blunts going. The crew was fresh to death in crisp white tees which read 'KFB', black Evisu jeans, and white on white Air Force Ones. They were iced out, each sporting an iced out Floss-A-Lot chain.

"Y'all ready?" B.G. asked. Although he was the headliner for the night, he wanted to show them his support.

"Yeah, Man," Kev said, popping his collar. He was on cloud nine.

"Aight. Good luck, Round," B.G. encouraged as Chuckie Boms, Big Whitney, and Kev took the stage.

The crowd went crazy as their local hit, "It's Nothin'" began playing. E-Way and Bubbles served as hype men. They were popping bottles of Cristal and throwing twenties into the crowd. They performed a total of eight songs, ending their set with their new song, "What Cha' Is". Skyy, Nicky, Tae, Erica, and Marie were all in the front row. They yelled in support as E-Way and the rest of them exited the stage.

"Come on y'all," Skyy said to her friends.

They made their way backstage flashing their passes at security.

Skyy rushed over to E-Way, giving him a kiss. "Y'all were great, Baby."

"Yeah, y'all did y'all thing," Nicky added.

"Oh my God! B.G.!" Tae screamed like a groupie. "Can I please take a picture with you?"

B.G. flicked up with Tae, Nicky, Marie, and Skyy before heading onto the stage.

Kev, Chuckie Boms, and Big Whitney passed out CDs and posters from their promotional van, a conversion van that E-Way had purchased and had gotten wrapped with Floss-A-Lot records on it.

After B.G.'s performance, they all headed over to the River Rock for the after party. Only major-league players were in the house with the exception of a few groupies. Bottles of Cristal and Moet filled the table. E-Way had gone all out for the night. After the after party everybody was supposed to hit the after-after party at the hotel. Skyy and her friends had a V.I.P. booth. They laughed it up and enjoyed free drinks and entertainment.

"Girl, do you know this is the third time I've seen ol' boy in two days?" Skyy informed as she nodded in the direction of Mario, the guy from the salon.

"His ass is too fine," Erica said.

No sooner than the words left her mouth, Mario turned around on his stool where he was seated at the bar with another gentleman. They were both wearing suits and loafers. His eyes met Skyy's and this time she didn't break her stare. Mario excused himself and then walked over to Skyy's V.I.P. booth.

"Excuse me ladies, but I was hoping I could steal a few minutes with...your name is?" Mario asked, looking into Skyy's eyes.

"Skyy," she replied.

"I'm Mario. Nice to meet you. I would buy you ladies a drink, but they're apparently free tonight. Listen, I won't take up too much of your time. How'd you like to go to the Source Awards with me next week? I know we've just met, but I'd really appreciate your company. You can even bring your girls."

"First Class or Coach?" Erica asked.

"Mario Lambert?" E-Way called out. "To what do I owe the pleasure?" He had spotted Mario at Skyy's booth and wanted to see what was up.

"Just enjoying the festivities," Mario answered. "By the way, Man, y'all did ya' thing tonight. When are you going to sign with me?"

Mario was a music producer, a real one. He had worked with some of everybody and was looking to bring the glory days back to Motown. He wanted to produce KFB among other groups because they had a unique sound.

"Man, we already signed," E-Way said.

"To who?"

There was a brief pause before E-Way responded. "We on some independent shit."

"Do you know how much money you'd make if you went major? Millions. You've got my number, Man. Think about it. As a matter-of-fact, give yourself a break from the streets and fly out to Miami with me to the Source Awards. It'll give you a chance to see how brothas is really eating. Plus, these lovely ladies will hopefully be joining us."

There was a loud ruckus at the front door which stole the attention of E-Way and everyone else.

"It's time to go," Mario announced. "These niggas about to act a donkey. It was nice meeting y'all," he said to the ladies.

No sooner than he completed his sentence, gun shots rang out throughout the club. Skyy, Tae, Nicky, Erica, and everybody else with some sense got down. But not E-Way. He ran in the direction of the shots, upping a .44 caliber Desert Eagle from his waistband. He made it to the door to find Big Whitney crying and rocking back and forth while holding Bubbles' lifeless body in his arms. Kev and Chuck were in the middle of the street busting at the gunmen as they sped away in an Astor minivan. The two returned to the vestibule of the club where Big Whitney continued to clutch Bubbles while sobbing.

E-Way stood over them in shock. Gun in hand, he was unable to say or do anything as he watched his best friend lie dead. He refused to believe it. He just knew that Bubbs would get up. He had to. Kev walked over to E-

Way and tried to get him to take a walk with him. E-Way was like a brick wall—he wouldn't budge. By this time people were rushing to the exit, running and screaming as they tried to get the hell out of dodge.

Skyy was worried that something might have happened to E-Way. She rushed towards the entrance to find him in a trance. "Baby, are you okay? Let's get out of here, Baby. Come on…let's go home." She pulled him by the arm.

Police sirens could be heard in the distance. They were approaching a mile per second. E-Way reluctantly followed Skyy, still looking back at his best friend.

***

"What happened?" Skyy asked as she and E-Way walked into their house.

E-Way hadn't said one word the entire ride home. His cell phone as blowing up with calls from Kev and the rest of KFB, but E-Way didn't even hear the phone. He was zoned out.

"What happened, E? Who did it?" Skyy asked as she followed E-Way up to their bedroom and into his walk-in closet. Skyy kept pressing the issue.

E-Way had one thing on his mind—murder! He changed his clothes, dressing in all black. He pulled up two floor boards removing an AR-15 fully automatic and two extra clips.

"What are you going to do?" Skyy grabbed E-Way's arm as he attempted to walk out of the closet.

He spun around and slapped Skyy to the ground. "Bitch, this is all your fault!'

"What?" Skyy asked. She began to cry as she held her face and scooted into a corner.

E-Way inched towards her with death in his eyes. "If yo' funky ass wasn't flirting in my face I would have been at the door. And Bubbles would still be here!" he yelled. E-Way reached down and grabbed Skyy by her hair. He started punching her in the face, hitting her at least ten times. Skyy screamed to the top of her lungs. She couldn't believe this was actually happening. E-Way had never hit her. He was going crazy and Skyy thought that he was going to kill her.

E-Way drug Skyy out into the bedroom. He picked her up and threw her onto the bed and then just stood there staring. He was out of breath. "I'll finish with yo' ass when I get back. Clean yo' self up," he said, turning to leave.

Skyy laid on the bed sniffling and crying. E-Way had busted her nose and blacked both of her eyes. She was soaked in blood. She heard the front door close and E-Way's car start. She reached over blindly to grab the house phone in order to call Nicky.

"He did what?" Nicky asked when she told him the news. "I'm on my way!"

Nicky wasted no time racing over to Skyy's house to pick her up.

Chapter 4

E-Way and the rest of KFB met at the studio. They were drinking and smoking Kush, trying to cope with the loss of Bubbles. E-Way paced back and forth with a bottle of Hennessy. Kev, Big Whitney, Chuck, and Chuckie Boms were all seated. They were listening to some of the tracks Bubbs had produced. Out of nowhere, E-Way threw the Hennessey bottle as hard as he could against the wall. Everybody looked up at him as he stood in the center of the floor looking up at the ceiling. No one had seen who killed Bubbles. There was just a big commotion and then shots were fired. Kev and Chuckie Boms were able to let off a couple of rounds but weren't able to identify the gunmen.

"So, who was it?" E-Way asked.

No one said a word.

"You mean to tell me that niggas just pulled up, dumped my man, and ain't nobody see shit?" E-Way asked.

Again, no one said a word. E-Way continued to pace the floor while plotting his next move. "This what we gon' do…First, we gon' put a reward up for the name of whoever did it. We'll kill those bitches ourselves. Put the word out that it's a hunnit g's for information. If that don't work we'll just kill every nigga we think could have did it. What y'all waiting on? Hit the streets and find out who did this!" he ordered.

It was six o'clock in the morning. None of them had been to sleep. They all combed the streets spreading the word and seeking information, but to no avail. E-Way had to go and break the news to his grandmother. She had raised him and Bubbles. E-Way and Bubbles had been best friends since birth. Their fathers were best friends back in the day. Each man's father was now serving seven life sentences for a robbery gone bad. Bubbles' mom, Nancy, was found raped and shot execution style in a crack house when he was only six years old. Ms. Nelly, E-Way's grandmother, adopted Bubbles and raised him as one of her own. Ms. Nelly nearly had a stroke after learning of Bubbles' death. It killed E-Way to watch her endure the pain. His eyes began to well up and he became furious all over again.

***

Meanwhile, Skyy had checked into the hospital. Her nose was broken and her jaw was dislocated. By her being high yellow, she bruised badly. Her entire face was black and blue. She cried as she looked into the mirror in the hospital room's bathroom.

Nicky heard her friend crying and entered the bathroom to hold Skyy in an effort to comfort her. "It's going to be alright, Baby. We'll get through this. We always do," Nicky assured her.

"Look at me," Skyy sobbed.

"Son of a bitch," Nicky replied. He was pissed. No one fucked with Skyy and got away with it. Nicky was very protective of Skyy. He regarded her as a little sister.

The doctors ran a few more X-rays on Skyy and then released her, giving Nicky strict instructions to keep her in bed for a least one week. They wanted Skyy to come back and do a follow up. Her jaw was wired and she sounded like Kanye West when his jaw was wired. Nicky took Skyy to his house. He lived in Southfield, Michigan in a three-bedroom ranch. His house was immaculate. Nicky used one of the bedrooms as an office. The second was his bedroom and the third was the guest room. He settled Skyy in the guest room and ran her a hot bath with Epsom salt so that she could soak her wounds.

Nicky was playing Momma, waiting on Skyy hand and foot. He had called the shop and had Marie to cover his schedule. He didn't tell her that Skyy was jumped on because he didn't want it all out in the streets. Skyy was on a liquid diet since her jaw was wired. Nicky tried to get her to drink chicken broth and Ensure shakes, but Skyy just laid in bed crying all day. She didn't think her face would ever heal.

Four days passed and Skyy hadn't budged except to use the bathroom and when Nicky gave her a bath. Nicky hadn't budged either. He had declined two dates with Devin. Nicky was by Skyy's beside twenty-four seven. Skyy's cell phone was turned off and her voicemail was full with messages from E-Way.

E-Way had a feeling about where Skyy was, but he'd never been to Nicky's house. He went up to the shop a few times threatening folks, Marie and Tae in particular, to tell him where Nicky lived. They couldn't tell him if they wanted to because Nicky was very particular about who he let know where he laid his head. On E-Way's last visit to the shop, Alina's hating ass slipped E-Way a piece of paper. It contained Nicky's home address and Alina's cell phone number. Alina had gotten Nicky's address by running his home number through information. Nicky had been using his house phone to call the shop and the number was left on the CALLER ID.

E-Way hadn't washed his ass or changed his clothes in four days. His appearance was that of a deranged mental patient. He chain-smoked blunts and reeked of alcohol. You could smell it coming out of his pores. E-

Way pulled up to the address scribbled on the paper. He squinted at the house and was convinced that it was indeed Nicky's place because he recognized Nicky's Benz sitting in the driveway. He cut the engine and got out. He rang Nicky's doorbell like a madman.

"Let me see who this is," Nicky told Skyy, getting up from the love seat in the guest room. He and Skyy were watching *What's Love Got to Do with It.* Nicky looked through the peep hole and became furious. He snatched the door open at the sight of E-Way.

"Where is she? I know she's in there. Move! Let me in," E-Way demanded as he tried to move past Nicky.

Nicky wasn't budging.

"You hear me? I said move you faggot ass bitch!" E-Way yelled.

Just as E-Way finished his statement, Nicky dropped his ass. He hit E-Way with a stiff right jab, landing a solid blow to E-Way's chin.

"You bitch! You hit me you bitch!" E-Ways said as he laid on his backside holding his jaw. He was in shock that Nicky had really put him on his ass.

"Get yo' bitch ass up so I can knock yo' ass out again," Nicky snapped, his masculinity coming out of him.

E-Way went to stand up, but Nicky was on his ass like a dog in heat. He pushed E-Way back down and landed on top of him. Nicky was beating the sleeves off of E-Way. He was biting him and trying to dig his eyes out. Skyy heard the commotion and climbed out of bed. She ran outside and tried to pull Nicky off of E-Way but was unable to do so. Nicky's next door neighbor had called the police the moment the ruckus started. Southfield Police were dispatched and on the scene within minutes.

The police managed to pry Nicky off of E-Way, whose face was covered in blood. Nicky tried his best to repay E-Way for what he'd done to Skyy.

"I'm a kill you, Bitch!" E-Way yelled after the police pulled Nicky off of him.

Nicky was still going. The police had to hit him with a Taser to calm him down. They arrested both Nicky and E-Way. They took E-Way in on some petty warrants; he would bond out at the station after his fingerprints came back. Nicky was arrested on minor assault charges; he would have to see a magistrate in the morning in order to get a bond. Skyy contacted a lawyer for Nicky so that he would have representation at his court hearing.

The next day, Nicky appeared in court and was given a personal bond because he'd never been arrested before. E-Way had bonded out as soon as he was booked. He was out just in time to bury his best friend. All of KFB wore white tees bearing a picture of a smiling Bubbles. E-Way sat in front of the Sacred Heart Catholic Church smoking blunt after blunt and drinking Hennessy while listening to 2 Pac's "How Long Will They Mourn Me".

E-Way couldn't bear seeing Bubbles in a casket so he just sat in his car and waited for the funeral services to end. He felt as though he was still paying his last respects and that Bubbs would understand him not going inside. After the services ended everyone tailed Bubbles' hearse to the cemetery. E-Way again remained in his car. Kev decided not to watch his friend get lowered into the ground either. He and E-Way sat in the car smoking together and passing the Henny back and forth, not saying a word. Bubbles was the life of KFB. He had kept everyone on their toes. His loss was a blow to all of the KFB and then some. Bubbs had one daughter, Vanessa, who was four-years-old. E-Way thought about how he was going to tell her that her father was dead as she walked into the cemetery with her mother.

The remainder of the KFB met at the bar along with the rest of Bubbles' family. E-Way excused himself and went up to the studio. He thought about Skyy. She was someone who knew him and could understand what he was going through. He sat at the mixing board with his cell phone in his hand. He'd tried calling Skyy's cell over ten times but kept getting her voice mail. He looked at the piece of paper with Nicky's address on it then turned it around and noticed Alina's number. E-Way dialed the number and sat back in his chair as the phone rang. Alina picked up on the third ring.

"Hello? May I speak to Alina?" he asked when she answered.

"This is she. Who is this?"

"This ol' boy you met at Elite a few days ago. You gave me Nicky's address with your number on the back of the paper."

"E-Way, right?"

"Yeah. Aye, listen…are you busy right now?"

"I'm at the shop. I have two more heads. Why? What's up?"

"Shit…I was hoping we could hook up and go somewhere and chill."

"Is this ya' number?" Alina asked while she discreetly looked around the shop.

"Yeah, this my cell."

"Okay. Yeah…we can do that. I'll call you in a little while. Give me enough time to finish up these two heads."

"That's a bet…. In a minute…"

Alina and E-Way met downtown at The Renaissance Center. E-Way suggested it because there was a hotel located inside along with high-end retail shops. He rented a room overlooking the Detroit River and they wasted no time once inside of the room. They began undressing each other at the door. Alina knew why she was there—to get fucked and that was it. She wasn't really attracted to E-Way. In fact, she thought he was ugly. She wanted what Skyy had, period.

Alina wanted to leave a lasting impression, so she fell to her knees and blessed E-Way with some head. She sat in a seductive posture, barley holding E-Way's dick with her French manicured fingers. She mouthed him while looking up into his eyes like an innocent school girl. E-Way clutched Alina's long, black, silky hair, manhandling her head to his satisfaction. Alina reminded E-Way so much of Skyy that he almost called out Skyy's name. He caught himself as he began nutting in Alina's mouth. She swallowed every last drop and continued to knock him off until she got him hard again.

They made their way into the bedroom where Alina walked over to the balcony and slide the doors open. She stepped outside butt-ass naked and motioned with her index finger for E-Way to join her. No one could see them because the room sat up so high. Alina climbed on top of a table situated on the balcony next to the railing. Her ass was hanging off of the table as she sat perched in doggy-style position. E-Way took the invitation, inserting his long, black, hard dick into Alina's pussy. She jerked and sighed as E-Way began fucking her brains out. Alina moaned and squirmed while holding onto the railing of the balcony. The sun was out and E-Way's black skin was dripping with sweat. He was about to nut so he pulled out and forced himself into Alina's tight, yellow asshole. He wanted her to feel the pain that he was feeling.

They continued to fuck all afternoon. E-Way hit Alina in every position possible. Whenever he finally bust a nut, she'd suck him back hard. For Alina, this was payback for every time Skyy shined on her. She didn't just want this to be a one-time thing. Alina wanted to fuck E-Way on the regular so every time she smiled in Skyy's face she'd think about her secret trysts with Skyy's man.

~ Chapter 5 ~

Word had gotten back as to who had killed Bubbles by a little nigga who was parked outside of the club that night trying to parking lot pimp because he wasn't on the A-list. He supposedly had seen the whole thing. He pulled off after the gunshots ceased, but had heard about the hundred thousand that was up for grabs. He didn't know Bubbles or the rest of KFB personally, but he knew where the studio was. He ran down all of what he'd seen to the best of his memory to Kev, E-Way, Chuck, Big Whitney, and Chuckie Boms. They were all sitting in the studio hanging on the young man's every word.

"Are you sure about this? Don't be lying, Lil Nigga," E-Way advised, trying to read whether or not the nigga was telling the truth or not.

"I wouldn't make up no shit like that. I'm telling you…it was DJ and Marcus," the lil' nigga said.

DJ and Marcus were the head niggas of Murkland Niggas, KFB's arch enemies.

"Who else did you tell about this?" E-Way asked.

"Nobody. I didn't even know who got killed until the word spread. That's when I heard about the reward."

"Aight then, Lil Nigga. Good looking out."

"What about the money?" the lil man asked, whose name was actually Dave.

"Oh…Kev gon' take care of you," E-Way informed him.

E-Way nodded and Kev stood up.

"Come on, Lil Nigga. Follow me," Kev said. He and Dave walked downstairs into the bar.

"How did I do?" Dave asked.

"You did good. Almost too good," Kev answered as he pulled a .38 revolver from underneath his shirt.

Boom, boom! Kev gave Dave two face shots and then stood over him emptying the remaining four shells into the boy's neck and stomach.

E-Way was upstairs orchestrating the move they were about to make on Murkland Niggas. Big Whitney, Chuck, and Chuckie Boms all listened intently to their parts.

"Big Whitney gon' drive while the rest of us jump out and air that bitch out. I don't give a fuck who's out there…kids, old folks, mommas, grandmommas. I don't give a fuck! You air they asses out too!" E-Way instructed.

There was no time to waste. E-Way wanted immediate gratification. He was so amped that he wasn't on his square. He was acting out of emotion.

He sent Kev to steal a van for the job. Kev was an expert at stealing cars. He used to come through the hood every morning in a different 'stoly' as they called them. He would give everyone a ride to school and then continue to joy ride until the police snatched him up. Kev stole a triple black conversion van. It was similar to their promotional van. He hit the horn three times as he pulled in front of the bar.

E-Way walked over to the window of the studio and peeked out. "That nigga still got it," he said.

"Who that?" Chuck asked.

"Kev. He got the van. Y'all niggas ready?"

No one said anything. They all filed downstairs out of the bar and hopped into the van. Kev had their latest CD playing as he punched it up Mt. Elliott. They were blowing blunts, trying to get their heads right. E-Way was all business. He turned down the radio as he spotted Marcus, DJ, and the rest of Murkland Niggas posted on the corner of Bloom and Emery.

"There them hoe ass niggas go right there," Kev pointed out.

Everyone sat up in attempt to get a visual.

"Kev, lay your seat back and just keep riding," E-Way directed as he climbed into the back with everyone else. "Go around the corner so you and Whitney can switch seats."

It was broad daylight. Kids were playing in their front lawns with the water hose. Old folks sat on the porch and the hoodlums lined the block trying to make a few sales.

"Whit, when you get to the corner just stop," E-Way said from the backseat.

E-Way, Kev, Chuck, and Chuckie Boms were clutching the door handles, waiting for the van to stop.

DJ noticed the van for the second time and asked Marcus, "Who this van keep circling the hood?"

"I don't know. Probably the hook," Marcus answered.

Everyone's attention was now focused on the van as it inched towards the corner. As soon as the van stopped everyone on the corner took off running in different directions. E-Way, Kev, Chuck, and Chuckie Boms hit the doors wearing black hoody sweaters pulled down over their eyes. Each carried fully automatic AR-15's. E-Way was focused on Marcus who had cut through a vacant lot. He gave chase while busting multiple rounds at Marcus. He struck Marcus in the back as he attempted to jump a privacy fence. The impact from the bullet sent Marcus flying over the fence and landing on his face in the alley.

E-Way leaped over the fence to find Marcus crawling and leaking badly. E-Way kicked Marcus in his side. "Roll yo' bitch ass over!" He continued to kick Marcus until he rolled over. He wanted Marcus to look him in the eyes so he'd know who killed him.

E-Way snatched his hoody off of his head and watched as Marcus' eyes widened. Before he could speak, E-Way aimed the rifle at his head and held the trigger back, emptying the clip. E-Way stood there still dissatisfied. If he could have he would have killed Marcus again. That's how fucked up he was over Bubbles' death.

The horn of the van broke E-Way from his trance. Big Whitney had spotted E-Way standing in the middle of the alley. E-Way turned and began running down the alley until he reached the van. Big Whitney peeled off, checking his rearview mirror until crossing 7 Mile into familiar territory.

"Did y'all get DJ's ass?" E-Way asked excitedly as he turned around in his seat.

"You know I got that bitch," Kev answered, taking a hit from his blunt.

E-Way smiled and began to relax. Chuck and Chuckie Boms had laid down a total of seven niggas, including Blood, Marcus' father. E-Way was finally returning to his normal self. He'd gotten the closure he wanted. Kev ditched the van while everyone else jumped into their own cars and went their separate ways. E-Way rode in the direction of the salon as he called Skyy's cell phone. It went straight to her voice mail. He started to leave a message, but didn't know what to say. He hung up and continued to drive on to the shop. He was hoping Skyy's car would be in its spot, but the spot was vacant. He continued riding down 7 Mile thinking of ways he could get Skyy back.

***

Meanwhile, Skyy was still at Nicky's house. She had just had the wire removed from her jaw and the color was beginning to return to her face. She and Nicky were sitting at the kitchen table playing two hand spades. Nicky was winning as usual.

"You know you can stay here as long as you want to, Skyy," Nicky said as he looked into her eyes. He could always tell when something was bothering Skyy because she would clam up and not say much.

"I know, but I'm not sure what I'm going to do," Skyy said honestly. "I'm not even sure what it is I want anymore, Nicky."

"I'll tell you what I'd do. I'd leave his ass and find me a nigga who appreciates my ass."

"I know, but it's not that easy."

"Once a nigga starts putting his dick beaters on you it'll never cease. He'll come apologizing with flowers and a card until the next time. You my girl no matter what and I got your back either way. I just don't want to see anything happen to yo' ass."

"Thank you, Nicky."

"Aight, Girl. Call me if you need anything," Nicky said, getting up from the table. I'm about to go get me some dick."

Skyy laughed. "I'm good."

Deep down Skyy knew that she wasn't good. A part of her hated E-Way for what he'd done and the other part of her wanted to forgive and forget the episode. Skyy told herself that she would give things one more try and if E-Way was to ever put his hands on her again it was over. She packed her clothes, cleaned the guest room, and then wrote Nicky a short thank you note. Skyy took a cab home. She noticed that E-Way's car was parked in the driveway. That was a first. E-Way would usually still be out running the streets. Skyy paid the driver and then lugged her bags through the front door.

E-Way heard the front door slam shut and jumped to his feet. He grabbed his pistol and crept towards the front room. Skyy sat her bags down and started walking through the kitchen.

"Matt, are you home?" Skyy called out.

E-Way relaxed at the sound of Skyy's voice. He tucked his pistol away and then took a deep breath. He and Skyy ran into each other in the kitchen. Neither of them said a word. Skyy was reading E-Way's body language. *He looks sorry*, she told herself.

E-Way didn't know what to say. He looked at Skyy's still bruised face and his eyes began to well up. He walked over to Skyy and took her into his arms. He rubbed her hair and kept telling her how sorry he was and that it'll never happen again. Skyy believed every word that E-Way said. She wanted things to work between them and was willing to try again. She felt a bit of a debt to E-Way, the same as she felt towards Nicky. E-Way had been there for her at times when she couldn't manage on her own.

"How was the funeral?" she asked, breaking the silence. She was trying to lighten up the mood.

"I didn't go. Well, I went...I just couldn't go inside. I couldn't stand to see Bubbs in no damn casket."

"I'm sorry, Baby. Are you okay?"

"I'm alright. I should be the one apologizing. Baby, I promise not to ever take things out on you. Bubbs' death wasn't your fault. It was just his time to go."

They embraced again with Skyy nestled against E-Way's chest.

"Are you hungry?" she asked, looking up into his eyes.

"Nah, I'm good. I'm just glad you back home. Come on...follow me," he said, grabbing Skyy by the hand.

He led her into the bathroom and began running a bath. He lit some scented candles which surrounded the tub and then began to undress Skyy while kissing her. This was the first time in a long time that E-Way had done something romantic. He turned on a slow jams CD. LSG was playing. He undressed himself and climbed into the tub after Skyy. E-Way bathed Skyy like a baby. He washed her feet, back, legs, and arms, and then gave her a deep massage all over starting at her temples and working his way back down to her feet.

"So a bitch gotta get whooped up to get some affection, huh?" Skyy laughed as she enjoyed the massage.

"Baby, you deserve it. You been deserved it and I promise to start being more affectionate."

"Mmmhmm. Just don't stop." Skyy closed her eyes. She knew that E-Way wasn't the romantic type, but she would take what she could get whenever she could get it.

~ Chapter 6 ~

After about a week of E-Way playing Prince Charming, shit got old. He was missing the streets and Skyy was missing the salon and of course her thang-thang, Chris. Her face was back to normal and she couldn't wait to hit Henry's Palace with Nicky on Thursday.

"I'm going back to work today," Skyy announced as she and E-Way ate breakfast in their kitchen.

"You don't work," he reminded her.

"Yes, I do. I'm the manager at the salon, thank you very much."

"Oh...if you consider that working then go right ahead."

"Forget you." Skyy laughed.

"I was just joking. It's good to see you back in the swing of things," E-Way said. He was jumping for joy on the inside because this meant that he was free to do him.

As soon as Skyy left for the shop E-Way was out of the door. E-Way met with Old Man Frank on his yacht. Every so often they would sit on the boat and play chess. Old Man Frank would always talk during the games, giving E-Way advice about life and game he was playing on the street. It was like Old Man Frank knew exactly what E-Way was going through or about to go through.

"Life is much like chess...there's no room for error. You need to tighten up your circle and try to step outside it so that you may watch everyone in it. Matt, always remember that love don't love nobody. In the end, you're all you've got…Checkmate," Old Man Frank said as he sat back in his chair and smiled.

E-Way was still trying to figure out how Old Man Frank made his last move. He had never beaten Old Man Frank in Chess and as far as he knew, no one had. E-Way wasn't there for the chess game. He was there to absorb the jewels that Old Man Frank gave him. The game he possessed was priceless. He made you work for it though, always speaking in parables. It was food for thought. E-Way would smoke a blunt after meeting with Old Man Frank and try to decipher all of what he'd said. He had a few beers with Old Man Frank and then thanked him for the knowledge before leaving.

E-Way sat inside of the studio listening to some tracks Kev and Chuck had put down. It wasn't the same without Bubbles; everything seemed dead. E-Way thought about what Old Man Frank told him about tightening up his circle and stepping outside of it. He began analyzing Kev, Chuck, Big Whitney, and Chuckie Boms. He realized that they were all dead weight and that he was putting out more than he took in. E-Way asked himself an honest question. *Would these niggas have done the same for me?* He couldn't honestly say that they would.

Gunshots broke E-Way from his train of thought. He and everyone else hit the floor for cover as bullets shattered the windows of the studio. Fire could be smelled coming from downstairs. The gunmen had set a fire using gasoline all around the bar. They knew that it was the remaining members of Murkland Niggas. They set fire to the bar so that E-Way and the rest of KFB would have no choice but to exit into gun fire. E-Way had been in situations like this before and had used the same tactic in the past.

He knew that he couldn't exit the bar at that very second but most importantly he knew not to panic.

E-Way crawled into the back room and retrieved a Mall-11 and an SKS. He tossed the SKS to Big Whitney who was slouched down in front of the studio's rear picture window. They nodded at each other and then jumped to their feet. There were two men out back and two out front. E-Way cleared the broken glass from the frame of the front window with the butt of his gun, nearly getting hit in the face with a bullet.

Big Whitney and E-Way were able to get the men to retreat as they let off close to a hundred rounds a piece. Once the men pulled off, E-Way opened the fire escape door and they all filed down the stairs. Kev, Chuck, and Chuckie Boms were all coughing from smoke inhalation. E-Way stood there watching his bar go up in flames. Kev tried to run back up the fire escape. He wanted to get all of their masters but Big Whitney grabbed him. The fire had spread badly and there was no saving any parts of the bar or the studio.

The fire department arrived well after the entire building had burned to a crisp. E-Way flashed on the firemen as they sprayed the ash.

"You bitches ain't never on time!" he hollered. "I bet if this was on the other side of 8 Mile you mothafuckas would have been there at the drop of a dime!"

"You've got insurance don't you, Man?" asked one of the firemen.

That only infuriated E-Way because he had just realized that he hadn't paid the insurance. The Detroit Police arrived on the scene and wanted to ask some questions. E-Way wasn't too cooperative with the police or the fire marshal. The police ran a gunpowder residue test on all of them and eventually arrested Big Whitney and E-Way. Kev, Chuck, and Chuckie Boms were let go after the police took a brief statement.

E-Way and Big Whitney sat in the musty 11th Precinct waiting to be seen by a detective which sometimes took three days or longer. E-Way called Skyy's cell phone. It rung over a dozen times and then went to voice mail. *Where this bitch at,* E-Way thought to himself. The turn-key had let him use the pay phone and was becoming impatient.

"I'm a try one more time," E-Way said as he dialed Skyy's cell again.

"Hello!" Skyy screamed into the phone.

"Damn, why you hollering all in my ear? Where are you?" he asked her.

"I'm out with Nicky. How come your calls say unavailable?"

"Cause I'm in jail."

"Jail? For what?"

"Nothing serious. Listen, I'll probably be in here for about three days until I see a detective. I don't have a bond, but just in case…call my lawyer and tell him to try to get me out on a writ in the morning."

"Anything else?"

"Yeah. Some lames burned down my damn bar."

"I'm sorry, Baby. I wish I could say something. That's too bad."

"Don't worry about it. Just handle that business and I'll see you in the morning."

"Okay, Baby. Bye."

***

"Who was that? You know we don't be taking any calls on our time," Chris said as he gave Skyy an exclusive lap dance.

"That was my man," she said.

"Who? E-Way's funky ass?" Nicky asked. "What the fuck he want?"

"He's in jail. Someone burned down his bar."

"Good for his ass," Nicky smirked.

"So does this mean I'll see you tonight?" Chris asked.

"Most definitely. I'll see you after the club," Skyy assured him.

"Girl, you got a fine piece of meat right there. You ain't sucking all that dick right. We need to do the watoosie tonight," Nicky said as he watched Chris walk towards the locker room.

Skyy laughed. "And just what the hell is the watoosie?"

"Me, you, and his fine ass. An orgy, Girl!"

"I think yo' ass done had one too many shots of Patron."

"Well, can I at least watch?"

Skyy laughed again. "Yo' ass is a freak!"

"Forget you then! I might have to take him home," Nicky leered as he grabbed a passing waiter by the arm. "And what's your name?"

The waiter jerked away as if he was offended by Nicky coming on to him. He shot Nicky a look of disgust and then kept on his way.

"You's a queer for real," Nicky shouted after him, obviously tipsy. "You just ain't had the right one bring it out ya' ass yet!"

Skyy was in tears laughing at Nicky. When he got faded everything was a go with him.

"Fuck this. I'm about to go get me some dick," Nicky vented. "I'm drunk and I'm horny."

"Where you going?" Skyy asked as Nicky grabbed his purse.

"Over to Devin's. I'll see you tomorrow. I want—"

"I know, I know. You want details," Skyy said, cutting him off.

"That's right God damn it! Details!" Nicky barked as he dug through his purse.

"Don't worry about it, Nicky. I got the bill."

"Aight then. You be safe."

"You too." Skyy continued to laugh as she watched Nicky stagger towards the exit.

***

Time had slipped pass Skyy. She'd stayed the night at Chris' and was awakened by the sound of free weights hitting the ground. Chris was in the next room running through his workout. Skyy rolled over and looked at the clock; it was almost noon. Her eyes bucked at the sight of the time as she remembered that she was supposed to call E-Way's lawyer. She scrambled for her clothes, desperately looking for her panties. *Fuck it*, she thought as she slid into her Eleven jeans raw ass.

Skyy ran into the other room to let Chris know that she was leaving. "How come you let me sleep so late?" she complained.

"You looked so peaceful. I didn't want to wake you."

"I'll see you later, okay?"

"Do we have time for a quickie?"

Skyy was tempted by his offer as she stared at Chris' sweaty chest and arms. She shook her head, snapping out of the day dream. "Later," she promised, giving him a kiss before leaving.

She punched her BMW down Woodward Avenue as she scrolled through her phone. She called the office John Glaser, E-Way's attorney while driving. His secretary informed Skyy that Mr. Glaser had already been to see E-Way and that he'd gotten him out on a writ.

"Shit!" Skyy said before thanking the secretary.

She raced home hoping not to find E-Way there. Her stomach dropped as she pulled into the driveway and saw E-Way's car parked in its spot. Parked at the curb was a Grosse Pointe squad car. Skyy noticed the police car, but didn't think it was much of a concern. She was trying to get her lie straight before going into the house. She looked into the mirror and straightened her hair before spraying perfume on her pants. She took a deep breath and then exited the car. Entering the house through the front door, she found E-Way standing in the living room with two white cops. The house was ransacked and glass was everywhere.

E-Way turned from the police and rushed over to Skyy. "Baby, are you okay? I thought you were kidnapped."

"Kidnapped!" she repeated in shock and then caught herself. "I came home last night and found the houses like this…I was scared so I went over to Nicky's for the night."

"It's going to be alright, Baby," E-Way comforted her, hugging her tight and kissing her forehead.

"Do you have any idea who could have done this?" one of the officers asked.

E-Way shook his head. He honestly didn't know because he'd never shown anyone besides Bubbles where he lived.

The police dusted for fingerprints and made a report.

"We'll be in touch with our findings," the other officer stated, handing E-Way a card.

"That's it?" E-Way snapped. "A mothafucka breaks into my house, violates my space, and that's it? You'll be in touch? Shit, I could have stayed in Detroit! It ain't no safer out here than it is there. Just get the hell out." He ushered the two officers to the front door and slammed it shut behind them.

Nothing was missing from the house, not even Skyy's jewelry. The burglars were obviously looking for something in particular. Whatever they were searching for it sure wasn't in the house. E-Way made sure never to keep dope where he laid his head and the bulk of his money was stashed at his grandmother's house. He was surprised that nothing had been taken and wondered who was responsible. He tried to tell himself that maybe whoever did it didn't know that it was his home; maybe it was a random robbery. But again, how come nothing was taken? It wasn't adding up.

Skyy was relieved that she hadn't been busted for her episode with Chris. She hurried into the bathroom, locking the door behind her so that she could shower. E-Way wasn't thinking two shits about Skyy and her whereabouts. It seemed things couldn't possibly get any worse for E-Way with the loss of Bubbles, the fire at the studio, going to jail, and now someone breaking into his house.

The house phone rang. It was E-Way's uncle, Toby. His grandmother had just been forced into the house at gunpoint by two masked men. Apparently, they slapped her around and demanded that she show them where the drugs and the money was at. She'd pleaded for her life and swore on the blood of Jesus that she didn't know anything about any drugs or money. The gunmen reluctantly left empty-handed, but not before beating ol' Grams. They beat her right into a coma. The next door neighbor had witnessed the entire thing.

E-Way couldn't stand to hear any more so he slammed down the phone. His eyes welled up at the thought of his grandmother laying in the hospital and being attacked. He began hyperventilating as he went berserk, throwing the remainder of the unbroken glass knick-knacks in the house. He ran upstairs and grabbed his AR-15 and then was out of the door. He called each member of KFB and told them to meet him at his grandmother's house. He punched it down McNichols, running every light that caught him. He was listening to Pac's latest CD Thug Mansion and was feeling every word that came through the speakers. E-Way's eyes were bloodshot red from the anger building inside of him. *Someone had the balls to put their hands on Grams*, he thought as he floored the accelerator. By the time he pulled up everyone from family to the KFB members were already there.

"Man, what happened, my nigga?" Kev asked as E-Way approached the front porch where everyone was gathered.

"Nothing compared to what's finna happen." E-Way then told them all what had transpired; how his house had been broken into and his grandmother had been beaten.

"You think them hoe ass Murkland bitches did this shit?" Chuckie Boms asked.

"Who else could have done it?" Kev snapped. "They the only mothafuckas we at war with."

"Yeah, but how they know where you live?" Chuck reasoned.

"That's a good ass question," E-Way said as he looked off into space. He thought about the possibly of the gunmen returning to his house and didn't want Skyy to experience what his grandmother had. E-Way quickly called Skyy at home and told her to leave the house and go stay with Nicky until he got things situated.

Kev went to steal another van. He was unable to find a conversion van this time so he settled upon a minivan. All of KFB climbed inside leaving their cars parked in front of E-Way's grandmother's house. Big Whitney, the designated driver, turned the corner of Bloom and low and behold the remainder of the Murkland Niggas stood on the very same corner on which seven of their homies had lost their lives. Teddy bears and empty liquor bottles surrounded the telephone pole on the corner of Bloom and Emery.

The men on the corner were like sitting ducks just waiting to be killed. It was a viscous game of cat and mouse but they called it 'beef'. E-Way wasn't focused on the group of men standing on the corner though. He instructed Big Whitney to stop halfway up the block. They pulled in front of a red-brick, ranch style house and parked. The house was packed with people. Little kids were running back and forth in the front yard and two old men sat on the porch drinking and playing checkers. The house belonged to Marcus' mother and late father, Blood.

"Kill every mothafucka in this bitch!" ordered E-Way as he, Kev, Chuck, and Chuckie Boms exited the van wearing hoodies and carrying assault rifles.

The two older gentlemen on the porch hadn't noticed the gang as they climbed the stairs. Kev blindsided the first gentleman, shooting him in his left temple. Before the second man could react, Kev flatlined him. E-Way, Chuck, and Chuckie Boms rushed inside of the house. There wasn't anyone in the front room but five women sat at the kitchen table adjacent to the living room. They instantly began to scream at the sight of the assault rifles.

"Which one of you bitches is Marcus' mother?" E-Way asked.

No one said anything; they just continued to scream at the top of their lungs.

E-Way figured that one of them had to be the mother so he just shot and killed them all. Chuck went upstairs and found Bootsy, Marcus' little brother, hiding under the bed. Chuck had seen his shoe sticking out from the other side so he acted as he if was going to leave but then fell to his knees and shot underneath the bed, hitting Bootsy in the face.

After killing everyone inside of the house, the crew jumped back into the van where Big Whitney sat waiting with the engine running. Kev shot into the crowd of men standing on the corner, hitting three people as they sped past. It was all out war and everything was fair game. E-Way knew that he'd have to move his grandmother once she was released from the hospital. The beef was too intense and really foolish because everyone knew where everyone's people stayed.

There were too many niggas to try to kill them all. The immediate members were dead, but Murkland was a hood thing just like KFB was, but only on a larger scale. Everyone was getting involved from young to old. That's how it was when they were in high school. Every time KFB fought Murkland they would always lose because grown ass men would come up to Pershing and jump in it. Old Man Frank had much respect among both sets and generations because he had that dust. What he said went. He would always get word to Blood, Marcus' father, to squash the beef. But it was a new day and age. He couldn't squash the beef even if he wanted to now. A nigga would slump his old ass if it was necessary. Still, Old Man Frank got word to E-Way that they needed to meet and E-Way knew exactly what the old man wanted—to give him another life lecture. So, Old Man Frank and E-Way met on the old man's yacht for another game of chess.

"Have you not been listening to what I've been trying to instill in you?" Old Man Frank asked as they started their first game.

E-Way knew not to answer. His job was to listen.

Old Man Frank continued. "Your chess game is a reflection of you. The way you move on the board is how you'll move in life. Right now you're moving without thinking. You've started a war that you're not prepared to fight. Look at the bar...I know that you let the insurance lapse. Checkmate!" Thought he called it, he was less enthusiastic about winning the game than before. "Look at me, Matt."

E-Way looked up from the chessboard like a little boy about to be chastised.

"Son, death is near. You need to consider leaving the city for a while," Old Man Frank advised. "I hope that you've put some money away. Take a vacation. Have you ever been outside of Detroit?"

E-Way shook his head.

"That's a damn shame, Son. The world is bigger than just the eastside of Detroit. I'm going to get you a passport. I want you to see that the world has a lot more to offer."

As always, E-Way thanked Old Man Frank for his advice and concern. He left the yacht and drove done Jefferson lost in thought. He couldn't stop replaying what Old Man Frank had said... *Death is near.*

Chapter 7

Skyy stayed at Nicky's house while E-Way tried to sort things out. Like any other day, she did her morning exercise and was out of the door headed to work. On this particular morning she had to go back inside of the house because Nicky had her car blocked in.

"Nicky, come move your car, Boy! You've got me blocked in," Skyy said as she pushed the door open to Nicky's room.

Nicky was in bed balled up in the fetal position crying.

"Did you hear me, Nicky?" Skyy asked. "How come you're not up yet?"

Nicky didn't response because he was still sniffling and crying. His back was to Skyy so she didn't realize that he was upset until she walked around to the other side of the bed. Taking notice of her friend's disposition, Skyy climbed in bed and pulled some Kleenex from the box on the nightstand.

"Is it Devin's funky ass?" Skyy asked as she wiped Nicky's tears before handing him a few more tissues. "Cause you know I'll fuck him up." There was a brief silence. "Nick, talk to me," Skyy pleaded. "What's wrong?"

Nicky tried to talk but only wept harder with each attempt.

Skyy felt helpless. She wanted to be there for Nicky for once and couldn't even support him properly because she didn't know what was bothering him. Nicky was always the strong one. He was always the one comforting Skyy after a breakup or if she was just depressed.

"Nicky, please talk to me," Skyy begged some more, beginning to cry herself.

The sight of Skyy crying made Nicky try harder to gain his composure. He sat up in bed and took a deep breath. "Skyy, I want to tell you something but I want you to promise not to flip out."

"What is it?" Skyy asked, wiping away her tears.

"Okay…Skyy…I have AIDS.

"What!" Skyy yelled. "Who gave you that shit? Devin?"

"I don't know," Nicky cried.

"How long have you had it?"

Nicky was crying his eyes out but was still trying to communicate with his friend. "The doctor said I've had it about three years, but I just found out about six months ago."

"How come you didn't say anything?"

"I refused to believe it. Plus, I didn't want you worrying about me. This morning I woke up and discovered these on my legs." Nicky pulled the covers back to reveal several lesions on his legs. "The doctor said that I'm in the final stage."

Skyy looked mortified. "What's the final stage?"

"Full blown AIDS."

"But is there something they can do?"

"Not too much of nothing."

"Oh, Nicky," Skyy cried a she took him into her arms. "We'll get through this. I'll be right here by your side. I promise. You hear me?"

"Yes," Nicky whispered through his sobs.

Skyy continued to hold Nicky as they cried their eyes out. Skyy couldn't imagine life without Nicky. He was her inspiration. Without Nicky the shop would fall to pieces literally. He was the backbone for a lot of people, not just Skyy. Nicky was the type of person who always protected those around him and would do anything to see them happy even it if was at his own expense.

Nicky made up in his mind that he wasn't going to be defeated by this. He told himself that he had AIDS but AIDS didn't have him. Telling Skyy was a burden lifted from his shoulders. He just needed to share the news with someone.

"Come on," he said to his friend, taking a deep breath.

"Where we going?" Skyy asked sounding confused.

"Where else? To the shop. We done cried and now it's time to smile. People need their hair done so let's make it."

Skyy smiled as Nicky got ready for another day at the shop. He had to be the strongest person she'd ever met. *That's the Nicky I know*, she thought. She picked out Nicky's clothes while he took a quick shower. He dressed to perfection as always with his signature neck tie and ass hugging slacks. He slapped on some Gucci perfume, checked his situation one last time in the mirror, and then was out the door.

"Why are you smiling so damn hard, Girl?" Nicky asked as he and Skyy rode to work in his car.

"Cause I absolutely love you."

"What did I tell you about love? It'll only let you down."

"Well, Nicky, you better not let me down," Skyy shot back.

Nicky smiled as he grabbed her hand and kissed it. "Have I ever?"

"No."

"Aight then."

The shop was jam packed as it was on any other day. Skyy and Nicky were greeted with the phony 'hey, how you doings', complimented on their attire, and then they went right to work. Nicky was running behind. He had two heads waiting. He handled the situation expertly as he directed Veronica, the shampoo girl, to take the second woman while he washed the hair of his first appointment.

"Skyy, there's someone here in back to see you," Tae informed Skyy. "She said she's your mother."

Skyy frowned and then stormed in back to her office. She swung the door open to find her mother, Trina, looking through some photos of a recent hair show. Trina looked up and smiled at her before putting down the pictures and walking over to Skyy who was still standing in the doorway. Trina attempted to hug her, but Skyy jerked away.

"What—" Skyy yelled, quickly catching herself. She closed the door and then finished her initial question. "What are you doing here and what do you want, Trina?" She'd always called her mother by her first name because she hated her and had minimum respect for the woman.

"I came to see about my little girl. Am I wrong for that?" Trina asked.

"Well, first of all, I'm more than alright. And as you can see, I'm no longer a little girl. But I forgot…you missed me growing up."

"Skyy…Baby, I didn't come here to argue."

"So why did you come because you're certainly not welcomed?"

Skyy was always short with Trina. She'd say something hurtful and then watch as the words took their effect. She watched as the verbal assaults crushed Trina's world. Not for one second was Skyy about to let her believe that she had the right to call herself a mother. Trina stood there looking like the true crack head that she was, wearing a musty white—though now yellow looking—tank top, a pair of ancient Guess shorts that had seen better days, and a pair of run down Nike cross trainers that now read 'ike'. Her hair was still its original length, the same as Skyy's, but it was matted to her scalp from many days of not washing it.

"Skyy, I need some help," Trina stated. "I'm tired of living like this. I want us to be a family again."

"We were never a family. Ya' left me, remember? I wish you would do the same right now cause you're crowding my space."

"Your father is sick and in the hospital. They believe he has multiple sclerosis."

"That nigga ain't my father and too bad for his ass. I hope he got insurance."

"Are you going to help me, Skyy? I would appreciate it very much."

"What do you want from me, Trina?"

"Help me enroll in a treatment center and help me through it. Please, Baby Girl."

"I'm not no damn drug counselor. You don't need me for that."

"Well…I tried," Trina said, throwing her hands up in the air.

Skyy became furious with Trina's slick statement. "You tried? Tried what? You act like a mothafucka supposed to just drop what they're doing and focus on you because you woke up today and decided you want to stop smoking crack. You're a grown ass woman. News flash, Trina, you're not a little girl anymore. Talkin' 'bout you tried. You need to try and get yo' ass up out of here and let folks get back to their work."

Skyy's mission had been accomplished. She has scourged Trina's ass once again. She watched as Trina dropped her head and then turned on her heels to head for the shops exit.

Nicky stopped her on her way out and slipped her a fifty. "Make sure you put something in your stomach," Nicky whispered.

Trina smiled and thanked Nicky before leaving. Nicky had always been nice to Trina out of respect for that fact that she was indeed Skyy's mother. He'd see Trina at the gas station from time to time and would always drop some change on her. Skyy hated when Nicky was nice to her. She wanted everyone to hate Trina as much as she did.

Nicky entered the backroom to find Skyy slumped down in her office chair pouting. "You okay?"

"How the hell she gon' bring her tainted ass up in here talkin' 'bout she tried? Asking me for help…"

Nicky just let Skyy vent her emotions as he listened. Skyy hated Trina because every time she looked in the mirror she saw her. That's just how much they resembled one another. Growing up, people would always tell Skyy how much she looked like her mother and Skyy hated it. Trina had never been inside of the shop before. She'd usually catch Skyy on her way in or out. Skyy felt like Trina was out of bounds for bringing herself into her place of business.

After Skyy calmed down, Nicky returned to his client. E-Way and Kev entered the shop and all eyes were directed towards them. Nicky caught the eye contact between Alina and E-Way. He broke up their obvious flirting by clearing his throat and giving E-Way a look of death.

E-Way laughed slightly and asked, "Where Skyy at? In back?"

Nicky didn't answer.

"Yeah, she back there," Marie replied.

Kev scanned the shop and caught the eye of a young lady getting her nails done. He walked over to the nail station and tried spitting a little game at the girl, but she wasn't feeling him. She looked him up and down with a look that said 'you're dismissed'. Kev stood there with the shit face and Erica's silly ass didn't help matters.

"Country Black, can't you see the woman ain't feeling you?" Erica laughed.

Everyone in the shop joined in on her laughter.

Kev had to save face so he went into boss mode. "You ol' bad body, bucket-head bitch. I fucked you already anyway."

"Bitch? Who you calling a bitch?" Erica yelled. She and the young lady whose nails she was doing both waited for Kev to answer.

"I mean, both y'all some bitches," Kev replied.

Erica jumped up and charged towards Kev, but Nicky intervened in the nick of time.

"Kev, you gon' have to wait outside," Nicky told him.

"What? You putting me out? I'm a boss! Bosses don't get put out. I'm leaving," Kev said, mean-mugging Erica.

"Get your Marvin the Martian looking ass out of here," Erica snapped.

"You just mad cause I ain't tried to holler at yo' funny built ass. You's a Floss-A-Lot groupie, Bitch," Kev said, exiting the shop.

"Who was that?" Erica's customer asked.

"One of E-Way's flunkies," Erica answered. "Nigga faking like he getting money. Fake ass, local rapping ass nigga." Erica was in her feelings because for once someone had roasted her.

"You sound a little salty," Alina commented sarcastically.

***

"Hey, Baby," E-Way said as he entered the backroom to find Skyy working on the computer.

"What are you doing here?" Skyy asked, surprised.

"Here to get you." E-Way pulled two first class tickets to Barbados from his pocket and handed them to Skyy.

"Barbados!" Skyy gasped.

"That's right, Baby. I told you we would spend more time together. Our flight leaves in a few hours so I need you to go home and pack a bag. We'll go shopping when the plane lands.

Skyy jumped to her feet, forgetting about what she was doing on the computer. She grabbed her purse, kissed E-Way, and then raced out of the door.

"Where you going, Girl? You grinning from ear to ear," Nicky piped up.

"Bitch, I'm going to Barbados," Skyy answered, showing Nicky the tickets.

E-Way made his way back to the front. Alina mean-mugged him from head to toe. She had the shit face.

"'Bout time you stepped your game up," Nicky said, rolling his eyes at E-Way. "Aight, Miss Thang. Send me a post card," Nicky instructed as Skyy and E-Way made their exit.

E-Way dropped Kev off and then headed home so that he and Skyy could pack a few things. E-Way hadn't bothered to tell anyone, with the exception of Old Man Frank, that he was leaving. Kev and the rest of KFB were under the impression that E-Way was going to re-up the next day since they were all just about out of drugs. E-Way hadn't thought much about selling drugs. He just needed to get away for a minute and clear his head. The trip was scheduled for four days and five nights.

Skyy had a window seat on the plane while E-Way laid across her lap like a baby.

"Wake me up when the plane lands," he told her.

So Skyy enjoyed the view and compliments of first class. She sipped several glasses of Cristal and enjoyed two bite-sized steaks. She'd never been out of the country and felt like a little girl on a field trip. The only traveling she had ever done had been with Nicky for hair shows. She'd been to Chicago, Atlanta, Miami, Vegas and a few other major cities but who hadn't? *It's not every day that a bitch goes to Barbados,* she told herself.

Skyy kissed E-Way on his cheek to awaken him.

"We there already?" he asked.

"No, sleepy head. I'm just happy and thankful, that's all."

E-Way smiled and drifted back to sleep.

Skyy had the best of both worlds, so she thought. With E-Way she had stability and comfort. With Chris she had companionship. Everything that E-Way lacked she found in Chris and vice versa. Together she had the perfect man.

After two movies and about ten glasses of champagne, the plane finally touched down in beautiful Barbados. Skyy absorbed every detail as the plane screeched to a stop at Barbados Airport. Beaches with white sand could be seen within walking distance. E-Way and Skyy took a shuttle to the Four Seasons Hotel about two miles from the airport. Old Man Frank had already booked them a suite overlooking the ocean. He'd suggested Barbados to E-Way because it was one of his favorite get-a-ways. Since the

70's Old Man Frank had been a regular tourist, taking his young thangs there for rendezvouses.

Skyy raced over to the balcony of their suite and opened the sliding screen doors. She nearly lost her breath at the sight of the sparkling blue water. The tranquility of the place overwhelmed Skyy. She was speechless. The ambiance was a much different scene from the hustle and bustle she was use to in Detroit. She walked out onto the balcony and took a deep breath and then exhaled with her eyes closed.

E-Way joined her. He was carrying two champagne glasses and bucket of chilled Rosette.

"Aren't you just Mr. Romantic?" Skyy asked, taking one of the glasses.

E-Way poured her up a drink and then poured one for himself. "Here's to us," he said, downing his cocktail.

E-Way's toast gave Skyy mixed feelings. She was happy to be there with him and couldn't imagine herself being there with anyone other than E-Way. But, when E-Way said 'to us', Skyy knew deep down that those were just words. She began to feel guilty about her late night trysts with Chris. She tried to justify her dealings by telling herself that E-Way had cheated on her too, although she'd never caught him red handed but she knew.

Just enjoy the moment, Skyy told herself. She refilled her glass and began to relax. E-Way ushered her over to a chaise lounge next to the railing of the balcony. Skyy laid across the sofa and E-Way took a seat at the end. He lifted Skyy's feet into his lap and removed her heels before massaging her right foot starting with the arch.

"Oohhh…ahhhh," Skyy sighed in satisfaction.

E-Way applied just enough pressure to every inch of Skyy's feet. After the massage, he lifted her sundress and removed her lace panties. He positioned himself between her legs, putting them over his shoulders. He spread her pussy lips with both hands and began licking her clit. Skyy was frozen stiff. She closed her eyes and laid her head back while gripping E-Way's ears. He started licking faster with each moan that Skyy gave. As she began to climax, E-Way sucked down on her entire pussy, swallowing every ounce of her juices. Skyy greedily mashed E-Way's face into her pussy as she continued to climax. She jerked with every thrust. Her legs locked around his neck and she came like never before.

E-Way slid out of his shorts and boxers and then climbed on top of Skyy. He inserted his foot-long dick and began stroking Skyy while kissing her neck. E-Way took Skyy's legs and pressed them up against her shoulders so that he could deep stroke her. He watched as his dick slid in and out of Skyy's pussy. His dick was soaking wet and gleaming from Skyy's moisture. She moaned while biting her bottom lip and looking E-Way in the eyes.

E-Way couldn't last another stroke. He bust off a fat nut on Skyy's stomach and then slid his half limp dick back inside of her. They were both breathing heavily. It had been a good minute since E-Way had laid pipe like that on Skyy.

"Get it back up," Skyy demanded as she forced him out of her, sat up, and began giving E-Way head. After getting him back up, she climbed on top of E-Way's dick and worked him out of another nut. They went at it all afternoon until the sun set. The beach had been deserted with the exception of a few lovebirds. Skyy noticed the quietness and wanted to carry their escapade down to the beach. She grabbed E-Way by the hand and led him out of the hotel room and down to the beach.

The stars seemed as if they were within arm's reach because the sky was so clear. The water had a fresh aroma and like heated swimming pool, it was still warm with fossils sparkling below the surface like diamonds. Skyy removed her bathing suit and walked out into the ocean. She turned around and motioned for E-Way to join her. He dropped his trunks and ran out into the water. E-Way swooped Skyy into his arms and began kissing her.

They made love in the depths of the ocean and then again on the warm, white sand of the beach. For the most part, all they did was have sex. A brief intermission occurred when Skyy went off to buy souvenirs for Nicky. Neither Skyy nor E-Way wanted to leave Barbados. They dreaded the routines that awaited them back in Detroit.

"Do we have to go back, E-baby?" Skyy asked.

"I wish we didn't have to," E-Way answered as he packed his things. He honestly meant it and realized the truth of his words the moment he spoke them. He stopped packing his light bag and flopped down on the end of the bed.

"What's wrong, Baby?" Skyy asked as she too stopped packing.

"I'm done," E-Way said.

"Done? Done with what?"

"I'm done with all the shit I have waiting on me back in Detroit. I'm done with all the street fame, money…all that shit." He threw his bag onto the floor.

Skyy stood there wondering where all of this was coming from. E-Way put his face down in his hands and rubbed his temples. Skyy sat on the bed next to him and put her arm around his shoulders. She didn't anything. She was now lost in her own thoughts. If E-Way stopped hustling, how would he support her lavish lifestyle? She began adding up how much money E-Way supposedly had saved and it wasn't nearly enough to just up and quit. She began to think out loud. "So…what are we going to do?"

E-Way hadn't yet thought about that, but he knew it was time for a change. "I don't know, Skyy, but I'll figure something out. We'll be straight whatever it is."

Skyy didn't feel very reassured. She knew E-Way to be a drug-dealer and that's it. He had no other skills to her knowledge. She too knew that selling dope wouldn't last forever and that it was time for a change. But, money was needed in order to make that change. She told herself that E-Way was just talking and that once back in Detroit he would be his normal, drug-dealing self.

~ Chapter 8 ~

Back in Detroit both Skyy and E-Ways real lives awaited them. The shop was packed as usual as Skyy sashayed through the door looking and feeling fabulous with her bronze colored tan. She stopped in the center of the salon and struck a pose.

"People, people. Do gather," she said as she dug into a bag full of souvenirs and began passing them out. She handed Nicky a gold necklace laced with pearls and a matching tennis bracelet. She then handed Marie a beautiful seashell. She gave Tae an hour-glass filled with white said.

Alina stood there waiting on her gift.

Skyy looked down into the bag and then back up at Alina. "All out of gifts. No, hold on." She tossed Alina a bottle of tanning lotion.

Alina looked at the label and asked, "Lotion?"

"Yeah, you a little ashy. That ought to take care of it," Skyy replied.

Everyone in the shop burst out laughing as Alina stood there with the shit face once again.

"People, people! Please excuse the accent," Skyy stated.

"Damn, Skyy! You ain't bring a bitch nothin'?" Erica asked.

"My bad, Erica. You know you my girl. I tell you what…tonight let's hit Henry's Palace on me.

Erica was sold.

"What about me?" Joe asked.

"Oh, you can come too," Skyy assured him.

"So, you got jokes?"

Nicky excused himself from his customer and then ushered Skyy into the back room. "Details, Bitch," he said, pulling up a chair.

Skyy also pulled out a chair and flopped down. She was all smiles as she gave Nicky the run down.

"Well, you look like you got your swagger back," Nicky told her, awaiting more details.

"Yeah, I'm good. Except for one thing."

"What's that, Babe?"

"E-Way flipped out down there."

"He ain't put his hands on you again did he?" Nicky asked.

"No, no—"

"I was about to say…But go ahead, Girl."

"He's talking about stopping hustling and everything. I think the nigga's having a midlife crisis. Nigga go out of the country and don't want to come back."

"That's a good thing isn't it?" Nicky asked.

"It is, but it isn't. We don't have enough money saved for him to just up and quit hustling. A bitch needs Prada, Gucci, Gators, and what not. He doesn't even have a backup plan."

"Do you?"

Truth be told, Skyy didn't have a backup plan either. "Hell yeah. I'm gon' leave his ass if he don't tighten up," she said.

"That's the hoe I raised," Nicky co-signed, giving Skyy a high-five.

"Has Trina been in here while I was gone?"

"I haven't seen your mom since you put her out."

"She's not my mom and good. I hope she stays the hell out of here."

"Let me get back out here to my customer before that perm mess her hair up."

"You hitting Henry's tonight with me and Erica?" Skyy asked, sounding hopeful.

"Yeah, I might let my presence be felt."

"Aight now!" Skyy laughed at Nicky as he rubbed his thighs.

***

Meanwhile, E-Way got up with Chuck and the rest of KFB at the State Fair Lounge. They were all flipping out on E-Way because they thought something had happened to him.

"Man, you just up and leave without telling anybody," Big Whitney said. "I thought niggas got at you."

"Yeah, Man. On my word, we was going through there today if you didn't surface," Kev added.

Now that everyone saw that E-Way was alright, it was time to talk business. Chuck and Chuckie Boms handed E-Way a brown paper bag. Kev and Big Whitney did the same. E-Way had thought about not re-upping, but he told himself that he had to do it at least two more times in order to have enough money to leave the game alone.

"You know how much money we missing right now?" Kev asked.

"A couple of my custos started going across the bridge. I'm gon' have to call and let 'em know I'm back on," Chuckie Boms commented.

E-Way usually would have been in on the conversation, but it just felt elementary. He had indeed made a conscious change. The conversation was so boring to him in light of his new outlook that he decided to end the meeting.

"Since we're all here, I might as well tell y'all now," he began as everyone sat up at attention.

"What the deal, my nigga?" Kev asked.

"After we finish the next two loads I'm done," he announced.

"Done with what?" Big Whitney asked, dreading the answer.

"I'm done with the game. It's time to do something else."

"Like what?" Chuck asked.

"Man, you done lost your damn mind," Kev stated. "Ever since Bubbles got killed you been on some other shit. What about us?"

E-Way hadn't given much thought to the wellbeing of the other KFB members. Everyone was all ears waiting for his response. Kev, just like the others, figured that E-Way had enough money to get out of the game already and felt as though he was going Hollywood on them.

"I'm going to turn y'all on to the plug so y'all can keep doing y'all. More than likely it'll be Big Whitney who I introduce to 'em. The rest of y'all can get on through Whit," E-Way decided.

It sounded logical and fair. Everyone started to relax and Kev tried to lighten the mood.

"So, now yo' ass got aspirations, huh?" Kev asked jokingly.

Everyone joined in on his laughter.

"But for real though…you serious, E? I mean, you can always change your mind," Big Whitney said. He was lying through his teeth. On the inside he was screaming for joy over the fact that he would be turned on to the plug.

E-Way read through the bullshit and didn't acknowledge Big Whitney's question. He was wondering whether or not the plug would allow him to turn Whitney on. E-Way doubted it, but he had to at least try seeing as he'd just given them his word. First things first, E-Way had to run things by Old Man Frank since he was the one who plugged him. E-Way excused himself from the group and headed out to the Detroit River where Old Man Frank's yacht was docked. Sure enough, Frank was perched on the yacht in a lounge chair entertaining four young ladies.

"Glad to see you in good spirits, Pops," E-Way said as he boarded the boat. He always called Frank Pops. He was the only father-figure that E-Way had ever known.

Old Man Frank got up to greet E-Way. He was wearing a pair of Polo shorts, no shirt, a pair of Polo deck shoes, and a captain's hat. He was a bit tipsy and was in a good mood. "Y'all say hello to my son," Old Man Frank said to the young ladies.

The women said hello and then carried on with their conversation. They were all in bathing suits and heels. Old Man Frank had a no clothes rule for women while on his yacht, but it was a little windy so he gave them a pass.

"Which one you want?" Old Man Frank asked.

E-Way laughed at the man's boldness. "You's out of control," he said.

"I'm serious. If I tell them skanks to jump in that water, I bet they do it. Watch this." Old Man Frank removed a bankroll large enough to choke a chicken from his pocket. "I got five thousand for the first one who can swim to that yacht and back, but you gotta do it naked," he said, pointing to a yacht docked about twenty yards away.

The four young ladies all looked at each other and then raced to take off their clothes. They jumped in the water like they were on the swim team.

Old Man Frank laughed at the sight of them swimming nude for the currency. "The power of a dollar, boy I tell ya'." He took two beers out of the cooler and then handed one to E-Way. "So how was the trip?"

"It was wonderful. I started not come back."

"I knew you'd like it. What about Skyy? Did she enjoy it?"

"Yeah, I'm going to have to start traveling more often."

"Now you're thinking."

One of the young ladies climbed back into the yacht soaking wet, ass and titties everywhere. She wasn't fazed by her nudity; she was too geeked over winning the five grand.

"Here you go, Baby," Old Frank said, handing the girl fifty-one hundred dollar bills. It was all one big game to Old Frank. Five G's was like five cents to him. He was still amazed at how people would exploit themselves for a few bucks.

E-Way was contemplating how he could bring up the topic of leaving the game and turning Whitney on to the plug.

Old Man Frank interrupted his thoughts. "Boy, what's wrong? Why you off in space?"

"I need to talk to you about something."

Old Man Frank snapped his fingers and motioned for the young ladies to excuse themselves. "What's on your mind, Son?"

"I want out," E-Way answered.

Old Man Frank took a long swig of his beer and then repeated E-Way's statement. "I want out...you sound like we part of the mob or something, Boy. Ain't nobody forcing you to sell no dope. If you want out, quit."

"Seriously?"

Old Man Frank got up to get another beer and then returned to his nook. "Let me tell you something. What one won't do, another one will. If you were to die or go to jail right now, you don't think that Subi would find someone to replace you? Thirty years ago when I met Subi's father, Ali, he was already filthy rich. You know why? Because before me there was somebody else. The name of the game is 'get rich and quit before your ass is too late'. Shit, I think it's a good idea that you get out. Run, Nigga. Run!" Old Man Frank laughed.

One down, one to go, E-Way thought. "I knew you'd understand, Pops."

"Now we'll have more time to play chess and mess with these tenderonies."

"Just one more thing. I promised my crew I'd turn 'em on once I'm finished."

"Hell to the nah. Them niggas is crash dummies. Don't turn them on to shit. I mean it."

"But Pops—"

"There's no life after but! To hell with them lames. I told you they would be your downfall. When you leave the game, leave it altogether. I turned you on because *I* trained you. I knew you were going to make it. You can't save everybody, Matt. Do you see me hanging with a bunch of niggas? No! And I never have. It's not my style and it ain't player-like. Niggas always think you owe 'em something." Old Frank downed his beer and then slammed the can down on the table.

"Pops, I didn't mean to upset you."

"I'm not upset. I just want you to start moving liked a seasoned vet. You know what your problem is? Your heart is too big. It's going to be the death of you. You watch and see." Old Frank had enough. He got up and walked into the cabin where the young ladies were, leaving E-Way out on the deck.

E-Way sipped his beer and watched the boats as they passed. He thought about all that Old Man Frank had said and his promise to his boys. Whatever Old Man Frank said usually went so E-Way decided that they would have to find their own connect. He wasn't about to go against Old Man Frank's instructions because he was one of the two people whom E-Way listened to—there was Old Man Frank and his grandmother; his confidantes.

***

Skyy, Nicky, Marie, and Erica all sat on the front row in their usual V.I.P. booth at Henry's Palace. They were geeked up and acting a donkey as the many fine brothas took the stage.

"Work that mothafucka!" Marie yelled. She was standing up throwing bills onto the stage. She'd come all the way out of her shell and Skyy and Nicky just laughed and egged her on.

"Spend that money, Girl," Nicky said.

"That nigga got an elephant dick," Marie said as she took her seat.

They all high-fived and laughed at Marie's comment.

It was a typical night out at Henry's. Dick was everywhere and the women were spending big dollars. It could be argued that women were more addicted to strip clubs than men. Reason being, women tend to get emotionally involved with someone in the club. They become possessive and reckless. A woman would take her man's money and give it to one of the steroid-taking niggas. In Henrys it happened every day.

Skyy excused herself away from the table and went to the ladies' room. On her way back she noticed Chris sitting with another woman near the back of the club. *He ain't on business*, Skyy thought, taking a quick inventory of the ambiance. He wasn't giving her a lap dance or trying to work her out of a dollar. No, instead he was extra close and was obviously flirting with the woman. The bitch was busted according to Skyy's appraisal. He could have at least been fucking with a dime.

Chris didn't even notice Skyy now standing over him. He was too busy cooing in ole' girl's ear.

"Chris!" Skyy yelled and then smacked her lips as if to say, "Really?"

Chris sat up a notch, but he didn't quite acknowledge Skyy how she expected him to.

"I didn't know you was comin' through tonight," he said.

"I can see that," Skyy replied, rolling her eyes over towards ole' girl.

"Chris, I didn't know you were married," the woman said in a tone that let Sky know that her statement was a lug meant for her.

"What, bitch? You tryna get cute?" Skyy snapped.

"Hold up! Who you callin' a bitch, Bitch?"

The woman went to stand up, but Skyy grabbed a half-full Moet bottle and slapped the woman across the side of her face with it. Chris disappeared into the shadows while Skyy straddled the woman on the sectional sofa and proceeded to beat the hell out of her.

"Girl, look!" Marie said, pointing towards the back of the club. "Ain't that Skyy back there?"

Nicky kicked off his shoes under the table. "Sho' is." He ran to assist Skyy. "Here, let me get the bitch!" Nicky pulled Skyy off of the woman.

Marie and Erica also ran to Skyy's aid. They took turns rag-dogging the woman until the bouncers came and broke it up. It was common for this sort of thing to happen on any given night. Damn near every night there would be some type of drama; whether it was two women fighting over one of the dancers or a husband out in the parking lot threatening to kill one of the dancers for messing around with his wife.

The bouncers tossed Skyy, Nicky, Marie, and Erica out into the parking lot. The woman whose ass they'd beat had to be rushed to the emergency room. Apparently, she'd suffered from a severe head trauma. Chris had disappeared off into the locker room once the madness popped off. He couldn't afford for the owner to know he was the nucleus of the matter or he would be fined. It was made known to every dancer when they first started that having a relationship with a customer was forbidden.

Skyy was in a blind rage. She was upset that Chris had tried to play her. She walked over to his brand new Corvette and keyed her initials into the driver's door. That wasn't enough damage, so she went to her trunk and removed a tire iron. Nicky, Marie, and Erica were already in the car. They were buzzing and hadn't really noticed Skyy's absence. They were replaying the ass whooping they'd put down just as a Detroit Police car pulled into the parking lot. Their laughter ceased and their high was blown. Nicky realized that Skyy wasn't in the driver's seat and he scanned the parking lot for her. Skyy was standing on the roof of Chris' Corvette hammering his windshield with the tire iron.

"What the fuck is wrong with this crazy bitch?" Nicky asked as he got out of the car and called Skyy's name.

It was too late. The police pulled in front of the car and flashed the light on Skyy. The officers got out and drew their weapons, ordering Skyy to get down. She complied and was promptly cuffed and hauled off to jail.

~ Chapter 9 ~

The next day Skyy was released from jail. Chris had told the arresting officers that he didn't wish to press charges, but they'd booked her anyway for public intoxication, disorderly conduct, and for basically wasting their time. Chris wasn't tripping about the car because Skyy had paid the bulk of the money for it. And he figured he'd just have her pay to get it fixed. Skyy had to explain to E-Way why she'd spent the night in jail. She couldn't say that she'd been at Nicky's house because Nicky had run into E-Way at an all-night eatery on Coney Island. He'd asked about Skyy and Nicky told him that they'd gone to the bar and got into it with some chicks only for Skyy to end up getting arrested.

Nicky picked Skyy up from the 10th Precinct early in the morning. He briefed her on what to tell E-Way so that their stories wouldn't contradict each other's. He dropped her off at home so that she could get her situation together.

"What the fuck you get arrested for last night and how come you didn't call me?" E-Way shouted as Skyy walked through the front door. He'd slept on the couch, nodding in and out all night, waiting for the phone to ring.

"No *'are you alright? I was worried'*. Just, what the fuck I get arrested for," Skyy commented.

"Don't play with me, Skyy. Yo' ass was probably up there fighting over some nigga. Don't let me find out you been giving my money to one of them pretty ass niggas. I'm a fuck you up!" E-Way had hit the nail on the head.

His words were so convicting that Skyy had to hurry up and flip the script before her eyes and facial expression told on her. "I'm not the one out here laying up," Skyy said. She knew that if she switched the focus E-Way would leave matters alone.

"Whatever. I'm not about to argue with yo' ass. I hope I made myself clear."

"Yes, Ike," Skyy replied sarcastically.

While Skyy took a shower, E-Way rummaged through her purse. He scrolled through her cell phone and wrote down every name and number on her recent call long. He wasn't the jealous type, but he was a man of pride. He needed to know if she was stepping out on him. *Why would she*, he asked himself. She had everything she wanted and then some. E-Way left the house and began dialing the numbers from Skyy's phone. He recognized most of the names because Skyy didn't keep up with too many people. He called them anyway though, just in case Skyy had disguised the names.

All except for one of the numbers was answered by a female. The name listed in the phone read 'Judy'. It was unfamiliar to E-Way. He had never met or heard Skyy speak of a Judy. The phone was answered on the second ring.

"Hello?" answered the deep voice of a man.

E-Way sat up in his seat as he drove to nowhere in particular. "Who this?" E-Way asked.

There was a slight pause and then the man said. "She ain't in right now, but who's callin'?"

E-Way pushed the END button, hanging up on the man.

The voice on the other end belonged to Chris. He was too swift on his toes to allow E-Way to catch him slipping. There was no Judy, but Chris wasn't about to let the cat out of the bag. He wasn't sure whose husband or nigga was calling, but he knew the game.

E-Way could sense from the man's pause that there was some shit in the game. He started to turn his car around and go beat the shit out of Skyy until she confessed, but he decided not to because he feared that he would kill her. E-Way turned onto 7 Mile heading west. His mind continued to race. He needed the truth. He flipped open his phone and called Alina. He figured he could easily pick her.

"Hello?" she answered.

"Can I speak to Alina?"

"Speaking." Alina rolled over in her bed still half asleep. It was going on eight o'clock in the morning and she wasn't quite a morning person.

"Damn, did I catch you at a bad time?"

"Nah. I mean, it's only 7:50. By the way, who is this?"

"E-Way. You done forgot about a nigga already?"

"I was beginning to think you forgot about me. You ain't never call me back."

"Well look, I need to ask you something and I want you to be honest with me."

"What is it?" Alina asked, sitting up at attention.

"Is Skyy fucking one of them niggas up at Henry's Palace?"

"To be honest, I don't know. I know that all of the girls at the shop go at least once a week…on Thursdays. And the next morning that's all they be talking 'bout. I don't go because I don't fuck with them like that."

"Yeah," E-Way said, lost in thought. "Well listen, do me a favor. The next time they go…when you say? Thursday? Go with them and see what's what. Can you do that for me?"

"I can't believe you. The only time you call me is to go spy on another bitch! You need to get with a bitch like me."

"Oh yeah? And what a bitch lie you can do for me?"

"A hellava lot more than what you're used to."

"Imagine that. But are you gon' do that for me or do I have to hire a private-eye?"

Alina thought for a moment and then decided to do it, not because E-Way had asked her to, but because of her hate for Skyy. She would do almost anything to witness her downfall. "If I do it, what's in it for me?"

"A hellava lot more than what you're used to."

"When can I see you again?"

"Shit, where you at right now?"

"At home still in bed."

"What you got on?" E-Way asked, trying to sound seductive.

"Just a t-shirt," Alina answered in a soft, little girl voice.

"Shit, give me yo' address and I'll be through there in a minute."

Skyy finished showering and was getting ready to leave out. She decided to treat herself to a day at the spa after spending the night in jail. As she gathered her belongings, she noticed that her purse had been probed through. E-Way was careful to put everything back how he found it, but she could still tell that he had been in her purse. Nothing was missing so she figured maybe he was just looking for numbers.

After leaving the spa, Skyy stopped by the shop to update Nicky on the current events. She was greeted with sarcasm by none other than Erica.

"What up, jailbird...I mean, Skyy," Erica joked.

"Go ahead. Laugh it up if you must. But please don't forget to cough it up. Yeah, that's right. It's booth rent time," Skyy said, holding out her hand.

The laughter ceased as everyone pretended not to hear Skyy. She looked around the salon and didn't see Nicky.

"Has anybody seen Nicky?" she asked.

"Oh yeah. He's in the back," Joe answered.

"See me before y'all leave," Skyy warned as she headed to the backroom.

She opened the door to find Nicky comforting Trina as she cried and wept. Skyy wasn't fazed by Trina's apparent grief. She looked at Nicky and then at Trina, asking, "What's she doing here? I thought I made myself clear when I said—"

"Skyy, now isn't the time," Nicky interjected.

"It really isn't. What does she want?"

"Skyy, it's your father. He passed away this morning in the hospital," Nicky advised.

"Okay? So, why are you telling me?"

Nicky jumped to his feet, grabbed Skyy by the arm, and rushed her into the bathroom. He slammed the door behind him and pinned Skyy up against the sink. "Look, Skyy, I know how you feel about your parents, I do. But, you need to show some respect right now. That woman out there is your mother and she needs you right now."

"Why are you always so damn nice to her? Where was she at when I needed her all those years, huh?" Skyy began to cry.

"This isn't about you right now. Sometimes in our lives we have to learn to forgive. Nobody's asking you to forget…just forgive."

Skyy didn't want to forgive and damn sure couldn't forget all that she'd been through as a result of her parents' decisions.

"I'm a let you cool down for a second," Nicky told her. "I'm a go check on your mother."

"Her name is Trina," Skyy said in between tears.

"Child, it's gon' be alright," Nicky said, leaving the bathroom.

He went back to where Trina was seated only to find that she was gone. The back door was open. Trina had obviously overheard Skyy and Nicky's conversation and decided that it would be best if she left.

Skyy came out of the bathroom after gathering her composure. She found Nicky locking the back door. "How'd you get rid of her?" she asked.

Nicky turned to face Skyy. "I didn't. She left while we were in the bathroom."

"Ain't nothing missing is it?" Skyy began to look around.

"I can't believe you." Nicky shook his head as he walked out front to tend to a customer.

Skyy hadn't thought twice about the death of her father or about once again hurting Trina's feelings. She flopped down in her leather chair and scrolled through her cell phone stopping at the name 'Judy'. She pushed the CALL button and tapped her foot nervously as the phone rang.

"Hello." Chris answered on the third ring.

"Are you mad at me?" Skyy asked.

"Nah. It's only a car. But it was fucked up how you put me on blast at my job."

"I'm sorry. Can I make it up to you?"

"And how you gon' do that?"

"However you want me to. I need to see you."

"How bad?" Chris asked as he began to rub himself.

"Really bad," Skyy responded as if she was getting fucked.

"Meet me at my house in twenty minutes."

"Okay," she said, hanging up the phone.

Her pussy was soaking wet. She raced out of the shop rolling her eyes at Nicky on her way out.

"Bitch, I know you ain't just roll yo' eyes at me," Nicky said.

Skyy didn't acknowledge him. She was on a mission. She beat Chris to his condo and sat in the parking lot waiting for him to pull up. He arrived shortly after driving a Chevy Tahoe. It was a rental, just until his 'Vette got fixed. Skyy and Chris wasted no time. Once inside they started going at it, tearing at each other's clothes in a rush to get naked. Chris swooped Skyy up and she wrapped her legs around his waist as he slid her down onto his awaiting, throbbing dick.

He stood in the living room facing a mirror which was mounted above the fire place. He watched every stroke as Skyy's yellow ass bounced in rhythm. She dug her nails into Chris' back as she reached her first climax. Chris then laid Skyy down on the plush carpet and stroked her from the side while holding up one of her legs. He looked into Skyy's eyes and could tell that she was about to have her second orgasm.

"Wait for me, Baby," he told her as he sped up his stroke.

Skyy couldn't wait; she was already there. She reached back and grabbed Chris' arm, pulling him into her.

"Ahhh!" Chris sighed as they came in unison.

They laid across the carpet, both out of breath and feeling better than ever. Sky began kissing on Chris' chest as she asked, "Did I make it up to you?"

"Yeah, you did that," Chris answered, still out of breath.

Make up sex has always been better than regular sex. Chris felt like he'd punished Skyy for what she did to his car and now he could forgive her. He laid down the law for future references in case Skyy had begun to think that he was soft and would go for anything. She agreed to never put him on blast again at his place of business.

That was all she wanted—to feel dominated and controlled. With Chris she got to explore that side of herself, but with E-Way she pretty much had her way. All she had to do was put the pussy on him and she got her way. There were a number of reasons why Skyy was fooling around with Chris. The number one reason was the danger and excitement of it all.

~ Chapter 10 ~

E-Way was finished blowing Alina's back out and was ready to hit the streets. She promised him that she would go to Henry's Palace on Thursday with Nicky and Skyy to try to find out if Skyy was indeed messing around with somebody. E-Way dug into his pants pocket and pulled out a wad of money. He peeled off five hundred dollar bills and then handed them to Alina.

She looked at the money in disgust. "What's this for?"

"Ah, that's just a little something," he told her. "It's nothing."

"I hope you don't think you just paid me for some ass because this pussy is priceless," she said with an attitude.

"Calm down. It ain't even like that. I just wanted you to have it. Do some shopping or something. I told you, fucking with me was a lot more than you're used to. I'm a get up out of here though." E-Way headed for the front door.

"When am I going to see you again?" Alina asked as he stood with the door ajar.

"Just call me," he answered before leaning over to kiss her on the cheek.

Alina felt special and victorious seeing as though she was getting it in with Skyy's man. Her new plan was to take E-Way from Skyy by all means. Even if it meant losing her friendship with Nicky. She wanted E-Way just that badly. At first, her fling with E-Way was just to get back at Skyy for always shining on her. But now Alina began to explore all of the possibilities; her imagination was getting the best of her. Just like everyone else, she had a hidden agenda.

***

E-Way met up with his connect, Subi. They always met at Pick-and-Save Grocery Store on 7 Mile and Van Dyke. It was one of the many fronts that Subi and his family had so that they could launder their dirty money. Subi was an Arab. He was the son of Ali, Old Man Frank's connect. When Ali passed away Subi was made the head of the family and the family business. He spoke perfect English because he'd been in America since the age of six. He was the perfect businessman. Subi could do four to five things at the same time and not miss a beat. Selling drugs and flipping money was in his blood.

E-Way parked his car near the docking area of the store and then walked around to the front. He strolled into the store as if he was a normal customer, walking through the meat section and then stopping at two stainless steel swinging doors. He looked around to make sure that no one was in sight and then entered the storage area. Subi's office was located upstairs. Glass windows surrounded his nook which enabled him to see E-Way as he climbed the stairs. Subi was on the phone, but he waved E-Way in and then immediately ended his conversation.

"E, Baby! What's up my nigga?" Subi asked, trying to sound hip and throwing his hands up in the air.

"What I tell you about that nigga shit?" E-Way asked, taking a seat in one of the leather chairs that faced Subi's desk.

"That's your problem…you're too sensitive, Baby. What you got for me?" Subi asked as he rubbed his greedy dick beaters together in anticipation.

"Two hundred and fifty G's" E-Way answered as he dug down into his pants and tossed Subi a large bag of all hundred dollar bills.

"Good. Come with me," Subi instructed as he tucked the money inside of one of his desk drawers before standing up.

Subi led E-Way down into the freezer and entered another freezer which contained nothing but drugs. Subi tossed E-Way a jar that held one thousand pills.

E-Way examined the jar confusedly and then asked, "What the fuck you give me this for?"

"That's the new epidemic. You're holding the new crack."

E-Way took another look at the pills and then handed the jar back to Subi. "Well, that's not what I'm here to purchase. Why you always tryin' to pin yo' get rich schemes on me? Tryin' to use me as a guinea pig."

"You paranoid, my nigga. What I just handed you will have this city going crazy in a few months. You just watch what I tell you. This called Molly. It's a combination of coke, heroin, and a bunch of shit. Your paranoia is going to cause you to miss out. Anyhow, help me with this crate."

Subi and E-Way hammered a crow bar into the top of the crate. After about seven blows the wood cracked and left an opening large enough for Subi to stick his hand inside of it.

"Am I getting paid for this?" E-Way asked as he leaned over the crate out of breath.

Subi held the crow bar while E-Way hammered. "My nigga, you're getting the best coke in all of Detroit and at southern prices. I'd say yes, you're getting paid." Subi began removing kilos from the crate and handing them to E-Way.

E-Way couldn't argue with what Subi said. The work wasn't stepped on and at fifteen thousand per kilo, he was making a killing. The coke Subi was giving him could be stepped on and almost turned into triple the amount. Each kilo was marked with a stamp with some Arabic writing. It was the Arab drug cartel's trademark. E-Way put the kilos inside of some brown paper bags and then placed them inside of some plastic grocery bags bearing the store's name.

Subi walked E-Way to the dock exit and watched him make his way to his car. "When will I see you again, E?" He stood on the dock with his hand underneath his shirt. He was clutching the butt of a semi-automatic .45.

E-Way tossed the kilos onto the backseat and then turned towards Subi. "I should be done in a few weeks. I've got something to tell you also but it can wait." He then jumped into his car and backed out.

E-Way called Kev, Chuck, Big Whitney, and Chuckie Boms and told them to meet him at Chuck's house. They all knew that E-Way had just copped, so they raced over to Chuck's to get their work. Chuck lived on Caldwell, a few streets over from E-Way's grandmother on Mt. Elliot. With all the money that Chuck was getting, he still lived with his momma. He didn't know how to manage his money. He'd spend it as soon as he made it.

Chuck, like most niggas, thought that he could sell drugs forever. E-Way copping was music to his ears because he was out of work and money.

Kev, Chuck, Big Whitney, and Chuckie Boms had all beat E-Way to the house. He pulled up shortly after to find all of their cars parked out front. He grabbed the work and then got out, looking up and down the block in search of no one in particular.

Chuck jumped to his feet and headed for the side door when he saw the shadow of someone on the side of the house through the basement window. He swung the door open before E-Way could do his coded knock.

"What's good, what's good?" E-Way asked, entering the basement.

Kev and Chuckie Boms was playing Madden on the PS2 while Big Whit rolled their third blunt. They all stopped what they were doing and focused their attention on the bags that E-Way was holding. E-Way walked over to the coffee table and dumped the kilos out. Everyone gathered around as he began to pass out everyone's ration.

"One more load y'all and I'm done," E-Way reminded them as they all gathered their packages and headed for the odor.

"Did you holla at the plug about me?" Big Whitney asked.

Everyone waited on E-Way to answer.

"Nah, not yet. I got you though," E-Way replied.

"Do I know 'em? Who is it?" Big Whitney asked.

"In due time. Let's get this shit pushed," E-Way said, changing the subject.

They all filed out of the basement and hopped into their cars to go their separate ways. E-Way decided to finally face his fear and visit his grandmother. He had gotten word from his uncle that she had come out of her coma just a few days ago. He stopped in the gift shop at the hospital and bought her a get well card, a teddy bear, and some flowers before heading up to her room. E-Way became teary eyed at the sight of his grandmother laid up in her hospital bed. Tubes ran through her nostrils and arms. She was resting peacefully as if she was still in a coma.

E-Way gently closed the door behind him and then walked slowly to his grandmother's bedside. He sat the flowers, card, and teddy bear on the night stand and just stood over her. He rubbed her silky grey hair while looking down at her as she slept. Her eyes slowly opened and she smiled at the sight of her boy, as she fondly referred to him.

"Momma, I didn't mean to wake you," E-Way said as he kissed her hand.

"It's okay," she assured him. "I was beginning to worry. I thought you weren't' going to come see about me." She managed a weak smile.

"Momma, you know how much I hate hospitals. Plus, I couldn't stand to see you in no coma." Tears threatened to cascade down E-Way's face.

"I'm okay, Baby. It's going to take a lot more than two street punks to get me out the way. The Lord ain't gon' let it be."

"Momma, I'm sorry. This is all my fault. I know this has something to do with me."

"We can't cry over spilled milk. It's done. Now we must learn from it and move on. Shit, they asses lucky I ain't have my piece on me. Every time I got my shit, don't nothing happen. Soon as I slip, here comes trouble. Won't happen again, you can bet that," Momma said, sitting up in the bed.

"Well, you won't have to worry about a next time because I'm done with that life. I want you to promise me you'll let me buy you a house once you're released from the hospital. I don't want you ever to experience nothing like this again."

"Boy, I'm not going anywhere. I'm a die in my house. You know how long that house been in our family? Damn near fifty years. I'm sorry, but I can't." Grams was set in her ways. There was no way she was going to let E-Way move her out to some quiet suburb. She enjoyed the constant happenings in Detroit. There was always something going on. She felt that if she moved out into the suburbs she'd die an early death from boredom.

E-Way knew not to press the issue so he changed the subject. "Do you remember anything specific about your attackers, Momma?"

"I remember the eyes of one of them. I've seen those eyes before. I just can't place it."

E-Way became furious as he visualized two men attacking his grandmother. It wasn't making sense thought. Grams had never met Marcus or any other member of Murkland Niggas. *How could she have recognized the eyes of one of the men*, he asked himself.

"So now that you're leaving that life, and I'm oh so glad, what are you going to do?" Momma asked, breaking E-Way's train of thought.

"I haven't figured that part out yet, Momma, but there's a million and one other things I can do besides selling drugs."

"That's the spirit, Baby."

"Aye, I have an idea. For starters, when you're released from the hospital why don't we open up a soul food joint? With your cooking and my business sense we can't lose. What do you say?"

Momma smiled as she considered the idea. It would be something else she could do. Plus, she loved to cook. "What will we call it?" she asked.

"How about Ma Dukes'?"

"I like it!" Momma's smile widened.

"Aight, it's settled then. Ma Dukes' it is." E-Way kissed Grams on the forehead.

Grams now had something else she could live for. Her entire life she'd always lived for others, from taking care of her siblings to raising her kids and then their kids. Out of them all, E-Way had always been her favorite. As much as it hurt her to see him out in the streets, she always supported him. When E-Way was in grade school he used to always get sent to the principal's office, he and Bubbles. The school would call Grams and she'd have to go pick them up. Kev, Chuck, Chuckie Boms, and Big Whitney's mothers would be going upside their heads while E-Way and Bubbles were on their way to Mr. Kennedy's penny candy store. Grans never whooped them. She always said that experience would teach them and there wasn't a need to beat them.

E-Way sat at Grams' bedside for most of the day watching soaps and eating white mint chocolates—they were Grams' favorite. The doctor told

E-Way that she would be released in a few more weeks and that she seemed to be recovering well. Grams drifted off to sleep after *All My Children* went off. E-Way sat next to the window in a recliner looking out onto the semi-busy traffic. The sun was beginning to set and the passing cars' headlights were glaring. E-Way watched the lights and thought about all he planned to do. He felt revived. He didn't want to just open Ma Dukes' Soul Food Restaurant. He wanted to challenge himself.

E-Way dug into the nightstand and retrieved a pen and a yellow note pad. He sat back in the recliner and wrote down a list of goals. Number one was to start Ma Dukes' and franchise it. Number two was to rebuild his studio and pursue a career as a producer. This would be done in memory of Bubbles. He used to teach E-Way everything he'd learned—he wanted to be a real producer. Bubbs had attended Specs Howard School of Broadcasting. Out of the group, he was the only one who had taken the music side serious. Number three on E-Way's list was to marry Skyy and have some kids. But, first he had to be certain that she wasn't stepping out on him.

Chapter 11

Nicky, being the true friend he was, took care of all the funeral arrangements for Skyy's father. Nicky went to Cole's Funeral Home and paid for the casket, suit, barber, and the actual funeral services. He also paid for the funeral home to pick up the body from the morgue. Nicky went all out, renting a limo for Trina and the little bit of family that Skyy's father had. He was sending Mr. Tobias out in style. The hard part was getting Skyy to attend the funeral Nicky vowed that he would get her to come, even if he had to tie her up and drag her there.

The loss of Skyy's father crushed Trina and any ambition she had built up over the past few weeks to stop getting high. To cope with the grief she went on a crack binge. Nicky combed the neighborhood in search of Trina. He wanted to let her know that the funeral had been taken care of and that she had someone in her corner. Nicky spotted Trina coming out of an abandoned house, which appeared to be a crack house. She was walking down the steps of the house with her fists closed tightly. She was high stepping towards a battered Honda Civic awaiting her at the curb. Nicky pulled behind the Honda and jumped out leaving his car running. He approached Trina as she opened the passenger side door. Nicky could tell from Trina's appearance that she had been getting high. Her eyes were bucked like they were fighting to bulge out of their sockets. She had a stench like no other. She was so gone that she almost didn't recognize Nicky.

"Nicky what are you doing over here?" she asked.

"I was looking for you. I came to let you know that the funeral has been arranged. It's set for Wednesday. It'll be at Cole's."

"You didn't have to do that, Nicky…but that's you."

Trina knew Nicky had done all the arrangements because had Skyy done them wouldn't she have been the one looking for her?

"I'd like to take you shopping so you can look nice for the funeral," Nicky told her.

"Child, you've got a heart of gold. But I'll be alright." Trina had one hand on the door and the other was closed tightly concealing her purchase.

The driver of the Honda, a four-foot Chinese guy, was growing impatient so he hit his horn. Nicky kneeled down and looked in the car and then moved Trina to the side "What the hell you blowing your hand at Chinaman?" he called out. "Mess around and get whooped."

The man looked nervous but said nothing.

"What's that in your hand, Trina?" Nicky asked.

Trina didn't answer. She just dropped her head in shame.

"Do you want some help, Trina?"

"Yes," she answered like a little girl.

"Then hand me that and let's go." Nicky reached for Trina's hand which concealed four dime rocks. Nicky took the rocks and slung them at the driver and then grabbed Trina by the hand and led her to his car. He put Trina in the passenger seat and then sped away from the curb, leaving the Chinaman bewildered.

"Thank you, Nicky," Trina managed to say as she began to cry.

"Don't thank me yet. There's a long road of recovery ahead of you, but I'm going to help you…but only if you help yourself. Deal?" Nicky stuck his hand out.

"Deal," Trina said as she shook his hand.

Nicky drove to his house so that Trina could bathe. The Lord knew that she needed two of them. He changed her into some fresh clothes. They fit just right seeing as though most of Nicky's clothes were female articles anyway. Nicky curled Trina's hair, sprayed some smell good on her, and then applied a little foundation. After giving Trina a Jenny Jones makeover, Nicky took her shopping for something to wear to the funeral. While there, he ended up buying her damn near an entire new wardrobe. Every outfit that Trina tried on Nicky tossed it on the counter. It had been ages since Trina had been to the mall to actually shop. The only shopping she ever did was shoplifting. She felt like a little girl in the candy store. Nicky didn't mind. He was getting his enjoyment as usual by making others happy.

After leaving the mall they stopped at Red Lobster where Nicky told Trina to order whatever she wanted. Why had he done that? Trina ordered and demolished a jumbo platter of shrimp and lobster tails. She ate like she was just released from a concentration camp. Nicky checked his cell phone messages. He had purposely turned his phone off. Skyy's name as listed as seven missed calls. Suddenly, he remembered that he was supposed to do Skyy's hair amongst others. *Oh well, they'll get over it*, Nicky thought to himself and then closed his phone.

"You 'bout ready?" he asked Trina.

"Now where we going?" she asked.

"Back to my house. I got a guest room all ready for you."

"Nicky, I would hate to impose upon you. I can't—"

"I insist and besides, I need to keep you away from Detroit…at least until we can get you into a treatment center. I told you, you've got a long road ahead of you."

"Nicky, I've been smoking crack since its debut. Do you really think I can shake this thing?"

"My mother used to always tell me, when you get tired of being sick and tired you'll quit. She was talking about me always getting in trouble. Trina, I know you're tired and yes, I believe you can quit. Question is, do you? Come on, let's get out of here."

***

Skyy was worried about Nicky. She drove out to his house to see if he was at home sick or something. She used her spare key to let herself in. She called Nicky's name at the top of her lungs as she searched every room in the house. Maybe he's over Devin's laid up, Skyy told herself. She wrote a note for Nicky, telling him that she'd been over and to call once he got the message. Skyy was looking up just as Nicky and Trina pulled up into the driveway.

Nicky noticed Skyy first as her back was turned while locking his front door. "Damn," he said.

"Is that my baby?" Trina asked, leaning forward in the seat to see.

"Yeah, that's her," Nicky said, killing the engine,

Skyy walked up to the driver's side door and began fussing at Nicky telling him how worried she was. She stopped mid-sentence as Trina emerged from the passenger side. Skyy looked as if she'd seen a ghost. She didn't even acknowledge Trina. Instead, she turned to Nicky for an explanation. "What's she doing here?"

"We had to get everything set for the funeral," Nicky replied.

"Here you go again. Nicky, you ain't Superman! You can't save everybody."

"You really need to quit, Skyy." Nicky walked around to the trunk.

"Who's all this for?" Skyy asked, referencing all of the bags that Nicky lifted out.

"Never mind that. Grab a few bags and help me carry them inside," Nicky ordered.

Skyy reluctantly helped carry the bags inside. Nicky got Trina settled in the guest room and then took Skyy into the basement for a scolding.

"I know what you're thinking, Skyy, and I know you're upset. But once again, it's not about you."

"You got her living in your house. Is you crazy, Boy?"

"I know what I'm doing. Skyy, your mother needs a helping hand. She really wants to change and I'm going to help her. After the funeral she's going to check into a treatment center. We can't turn our backs on her."

"*We* ain't got nothing to do with it. If you wanna run around playing Oprah and shit, be my guest. But don't expect me to partake."

"Anyhow, the funeral is Wednesday. I expect to see you in attendance."

"Well you can expect to be disappointed" Skyy headed up the stairs. She didn't bother saying goodbye to Trina. She just walked out, got into her car, and peeled off.

"She hates me, doesn't she?" Trina asked Nicky as he entered the room.

"Like all things, give it some time. She'll come around. Skyy is just being Skyy."

That was what Trina feared the most—Skyy being the cold-hearted woman that she was responsible for creating. She felt that Skyy would never forgive her.

It wasn't so much that Nicky was helping Trina which bothered Skyy. It was a mixture of feelings. Skyy for one felt like Trina was taking the one true friend that she had away from her. *What right does she have to impose herself and why is Nicky so damn nice to her*, Skyy asked herself as she drove like a mad woman, weaving in and out of traffic. *I wish she would just die and leave me the hell alone.* She began to cry. All of the feelings and memories of abandonment were starting to replay in Skyy's head. All the nights that she'd cried herself to sleep asking God why her life was the way it was began to come back and haunt her. What right did Trina have?

~ Chapter 12 ~

The morning of the funeral, Skyy laid in bed staring at the ceiling. Usually she would have been up, finished with her workout, and on her way to the shop. But, today she didn't feel like doing anything and she'd made up her mind that she would not be attending the funeral regardless of what Nicky said. E-Way was up and at 'em early though. He emerged from his walk-in closet suited and booted. Skyy looked on in amazement.

"Where you on your way to all G.Q.?" she asked him.

E-Way stood in the mirror checking his situation. He snapped his fingers and then pointed to himself in approval. "I'm going to pay my respects. You need to get up and do the same," he said, turning to face Skyy.

Skyy rolled her eyes and then turned over in bed. "You barely even knew my father."

"That's just it. He's your father and that's good enough for me. Now, let's go. I want to get there early."

Skyy didn't budge. She didn't give a damn what E-Way was talking about. She was a little irritated. Why was it that everyone seemed to be on Trina's side?

The doorbell sounded and E-Way rushed downstairs to answer it as if he'd been expecting someone

"Where is she?" asked Nicky, pushing past E-Way. He had decided to put their differences to the side and work with E-Way to get Skyy to the funeral.

"She's upstairs in bed talking 'bout she ain't going," E-Way reported.

Nicky looked at his watch and then stormed upstairs. Skyy wasn't shocked to see Nicky. She knew that he'd be there at some point to play Superman.

"Girl, if you don't get yo' spoiled ass up!" Nicky shouted, snatching the covers off of Skyy.

"I'm not going," she whined, fighting for the covers.

"The hell if you ain't." Nicky walked into Skyy's closet and snatched her down something to wear. "Here. Point this on." He tossed the clothes at her.

"You gon' just make me go, huh?"

"Yup. Now let's go! Get 'cha ass up, pull ya' draws out ya' cat, and let's go." Nicky clapped his hands as he spoke. He wasn't taking no for an answer.

Skyy reluctantly got up and headed for the bathroom. She showered and then drug herself about as she got dressed. Trina was waiting in the living room. Skyy flipped out at the sight of her sitting on the sofa. E-Way had fixed her some coffee and they were talking as Skyy and Nicky entered the room.

"I can't believe you," Skyy hissed.

"Skyy, now isn't the time," Nicky said, putting his hand over her mouth.

"Hi, Skyy," Trina said cheerily.

Nicky nudged Skyy.

"Hello, Trina," Skyy replied dryly.

E-Way and Skyy tailed Nicky to the funeral home. They were running late due to Skyy's procrastination. The service was just beginning as they entered the funeral home. A pastor from Word of Faith Church, Keith Butler, gave the eulogy. Skyy and Trina were ushered to the front along with Nicky. Skyy noticed that Erica, Tae, Marie, and even Alina were in attendance. They were all there to show their support but even more so because Nicky made them go.

Skyy felt betrayed and thankful all at the same time. No one else was in attendance. James, Skyy's father, didn't have family. He'd burned his bridges over the years, stealing from family members to support his high. Trina was his only family.

Pastor Butler said some kind words about James as if he'd known him. He asked if anyone else wanted to say something as well. Trina tried to stand and speak, but was unable. She just couldn't gather herself to do so. Skyy looked at her mother in disbelief. *She knows she's puttin' a ten on it,* Skyy thought as she watched Trina cry. *It ain't even that serious.*

The services were rather quick. Nicky had planned a gathering at his house afterwards but Skyy was too far in her feelings. She demanded that E-Way take her home. Once home, she got into her car and pulled off. E-Way called her phone immediately.

"Where the hell you going?" he asked her.

"I just need to ride around and clear my head," she snapped before hanging up.

***

The next day everything seemed to be back to normal. Skyy was her usual self—up and at 'em early and out of the door. She arrived at the shop ready for another day of gossip followed by ladies night out at Henry's Palace. Skyy held her head extra high as she entered the shop. She didn't want a bitch to see her down for one second. She was greeted by everyone as she made her way to the back. She was rather short with Nicky so he politely excused himself from his customer.

"Miss Thang, do you got something you want to get off your chest?" Nicky asked as he entered the backroom and closed the door.

"Why you ask that?" Skyy asked, turning from the computer to face Nicky.

"Cause you got your ass on your shoulders and what not. You needs to let that shit go."

Skyy took a deep breath. She hadn't meant to be short with Nicky. "I'm sorry. I know I've got some issues with my mother and I plan on dealing with them as soon as the time is right. When I'm ready, not when she's ready."

"Well, I think that's a start. When you're ready, sit her down and ask her what's in your heart without being hurtful. Ask her why she chose the streets over you. Ask her all the questions you've wanted to ask for all these years. Once you get the closure you need then you can maybe start forgiving."

"You sure know what to say, Nicky. I think you missed your calling. You should have been a counselor or something." Skyy could never stay mad at Nicky and vice versa.

"So are we on for tonight at Henry's?"

"Most definitely. I need to see my boo."

"Guess who wants to come!"

"Who?" Skyy asked, looking puzzled.

"Alina. She been asking me for the past few days whether or not we were going."

"I knew she would see the light…actin' all high sadiddy and what not. Anyways, I'm a let you get back to your customer. I'm a finish looking at these purses."

Nicky turned to leave and Skyy went back to surfing the net.

***

Skyy was almost turned away at the door at Henry's Palace. One of the bouncers remembered her from the incident the week before. She called Chris outside and he cleared it up, promising that she would behave. Alina was all ears and eyes, watching Skyy's every move. She noted how Chris paid intent attention to Skyy over the other women and how Skyy kept referring to him as 'Boo'.

"What's his name, Girl? That nigga is too fine," Alina inquired as Chris left their table to get ready for his set.

"Chris. That's Skyy's lil' thang-thang," Marie volunteered.

"What about Chris?" Skyy asked, overhearing the tail end of Marie's statement.

"Nothing. Alina was just asking who he was," Marie replied.

"Bitch, calm down. Don't nobody want Chris' high yellow ass but you," Nicky said before downing his drink. "Where the hell is that waiter? Now his ass is fine.

It as a typical night at Henry's. Alina enjoyed herself more than she thought she would. She enjoyed several lap dances by five different brothas. After just one night she was looking forward to her next visit. She could see how Skyy could get caught up with one of the many dime pieces that Henry's possessed. What woman wouldn't? Yet at the same time, that wouldn't keep her from telling E-Way all that she'd learned.

Chapter 13

Alina couldn't wait to relay her findings to E-Way. After leaving Henry's she called him and ran down everything she'd witnessed. She gave E-Way a description of Chris, his car, and the relationship had had with Skyy. E-Way became so furious that he slammed the phone down while Alina was still giving him the details. He was at home pacing back and forth in the living room. He'd been waiting all night for Alina to call. Now, struck by the news, he started devising his plan.

"Nah, that won't work," he said aloud at the thought of killing Skyy and chopping her body up. "Too messy."

E-Way continued to contemplate. His focus was broken by the ring of his cell phone. Speaking of the devil—it was none other than Skyy.

"Hey, Baby. Listen, I'm going to stay the night at Nicky's. I'm too bent to drive home," Skyy said with a slur.

This bitch trying to play me so she can go lay up with muscle man, E-Way thought. "Where you at? I'll come get you," he said, trying to hold back his anger.

"I'm on my way to Nicky's."

"Why he couldn't drop you off?"

"He's drunker than I am. The bar ain't too far from his house though. I'll call you once we make it home. E, did you hear me, Baby?"

"Yeah, I heard you." E-Way was lost in thought. He grabbed his car keys and was out of the door as soon as Skyy ended their conversation. He drove down 7 Mile. Passing the salon, he noticed Skyy's car still parked in its spot. He jumped on the Southfield Expressway, punching it as he came up on 9 Mile and Greenfield. Within ten minutes he was pulling in front of Nicky's. He called Skyy's cell phone while standing on the front porch.

Skyy and Nicky were in the kitchen recapping the night's events. Nicky was at the stove cooking breakfast for the two of them.

"That's probably Chris wondering why you left without saying goodnight," Nicky said in reference to Skyy's incoming call.

The call came in as unavailable. E-Way had dialed star, six, seven before calling. Usually Skyy wouldn't answer, but being tipsy and anticipating that it might be Chris, she answered.

"Hello?" she greeted the caller.

"Come open the door!"

"E-Way? Where are you?" Skyy asked as she got up and headed towards the front door.

"I'm outside."

Skyy hung up the phone and let E-Way in. "Boy, what are you doing here? I told you I was alright."

"Skyy, who is that?" Nicky asked as he walked into the living room. "Hmm," Nicky grunted at the sight of E-Way.

"Who was y'all expecting?" E-Way asked, catching them both off guard.

"I wasn't expecting nobody. Nicky was waiting on Devin to come over," Skyy retorted with an attitude. She was obviously irritated by his abrupt appearance.

"You ready?" he asked her.

"Nicky, let me go," Skyy said, giving Nicky a kiss goodbye. "I'll see you tomorrow."

"That nigga pussy whipped. He came and got that ass," Nicky joked as he let Skyy and E-Way out.

As they drove home Skyy could sense that something was bothering E-Way. She was sure that it wasn't a lack of pussy because when she tried to unbuckle his pants he pushed her hands away.

"What's wrong with you?" she finally asked him.

"Who you trying to play, huh?" E-Way asked out of nowhere. He turned to face her with death in his eyes.

"Boy, I don't know what the fuck you tripping off of, but you need to leave it alone whatever it is."

"Do I look like one of these suckas out here?"

Skyy's eyes were bucked as she listened intently. She was just waiting for E-Way to say it. Fear took over her entire body.

"Who the hell is Chris?" E-Way demanded to know.

Damn it! "I don't know no damn body named Chris."

"Bitch!" E-Way yelled, slapping the dog shit out of Skyy.

Skyy immediately began to cry. She balled up her hands to protect her face with her back against the passenger door. "You said you would never hit me again!"

"Ah, Bitch, that ain't nothin' compared to what I'm bouts to do to that ass," he told her as he pulled up to a red light. "Just wait 'til we get home."

Skyy's life flashed before her eyes. The jig was up; she'd been caught. There was only one smart thing that she could do—run like hell! She bolted for the door but was unable to get out. E-Way had put the child-lock on just in case she tried to run. He grabbed her neck and slammed her back into her seat.

"Where do you think you going, Bitch?" he asked, still manhandling her.

The light turned green and E-Way punched it, looking in all directions for the cops.

Again, Skyy's life flashed before her. She had to come up with something and quick. She started wrecking her brain. *Think, Skyy!* "E, Baby…let me explain," she pleaded.

"Explain? Explain what? Just a minute ago you ain't have shit to explain. *I don't know no damn Chris.* Now you see that ass is hit like good weed, you wanna talk. Go 'head, Bitch. I want to hear how you gon' try to come up out of this one."

"I do know a Chris."

"Okay?"

"But it's not what you think."

"So you lied to me. What the fuck you mean, you do know a Chris…like it's more than one Chris. You better quit playing on my intelligence, Bitch. You hear me?"

"I know Chris. He's a dancer at Henry's."

"So, this the nigga you been giving all my damn money to, huh?"

"I haven't given Chris anything other than tips."

"So you ain't gave this nigga no pussy?"

"Absolutely not! I only see him at the bar. E, I don't know who you're getting all this from, but Baby it's bullshit. You know I would never cheat on you."

E-Way thought about the credibility of his source, Alina. *She could be lying just to get in good with me, but then again why did Skyy lie when I first mentioned Chris*, E-Way thought. "If it ain't nothin' going on between you and Chris why you lie about it the first time?"

"Cause I didn't want to upset you. I know you're a man of pride, Baby, and I didn't want you questioning yourself. Women go to these bars to enjoy themselves just like men. That doesn't mean you have to be fooling around with someone there." Skyy was working her magic.

Skyy knew that she had to enter the house on a good note or risk the chance of another beat down. She reached for E-Way's belt buckle, but this time he didn't refuse her. She unzipped his shorts and then reached down into his boxers to pull his dick out. Skyy sucked him like an infant sucking its mother's tit. E-Way began to relax. He let his seat back and gently held

Skyy's head with his free hand. He was about to bust, but Skyy gripped the head of his dick preventing him from ejaculating. She wanted to carry things on to the bedroom.

E-Way fell for it as always. All Skyy had to do was put that priceless head on him and it was a wrap. They pulled into the driveway with Skyy still serving E-Way up. He was so focused on getting that nut off that he wasn't even thinking about why he was mad at her or his original plan to fuck her up. Once inside, E-Way took off all of his clothes and dropped them at the door. He stood in the living room jacking his dick as he watched Skyy undress.

She teased him with every article of clothing, taking her precious time. She knew that E-Way was ready to bust at any second. After she dropped her panties, Skyy walked over to E-Way and pushed him down onto the sofa. She climbed onto his throbbing dick, dug her nails into his chest, and then began riding him. She closed her eyes and leaned her head back as E-Way slid her up and down on his dick violently. After only ten strokes, E-Way reached his climax. But, Skyy wanted more so she immediately got him back up by continuing to ride his limp dick.

Skyy kept E-Way busy until the sun came up. He slept like a baby while she got up and was headed out of the door on her way to the shop. E-Way didn't wake up until one o'clock in the afternoon. He rolled over and patted Skyy's side of the bed and then opened his eyes, looking around the room. He looked at the clock on the nightstand and then rubbed his face, trying to gather himself. Last night's events began to replay themselves. He smiled at the thought of Skyy and their episode and then he frowned as he remembered what Alina had told him. He pulled the covers back and rolled out of bed. He grabbed his cell phone to call Alina.

"Hello," Alina answered on the third ring. She was at the shop standing right next to Nicky.

"What's up, Ma?" E-Way asked.

"Working." Alina nervously stole a glance around the shop.

"Aye listen, are you sure about everything you told me last night?"

"I'm quite sure. Why would you ask that?"

"I just wanted to be certain. That's all."

"Well, I'm not one to be making things out to be more than they are. I know what I seen," Alina spat out, copping an attitude. She was salty that Skyy hadn't gotten her ass whooped and now E-Way was questioning her credibility.

"Aight. You ain't gotta get all hostile. Look, I'm a get up with you later."

"Whatever." She hung up on E-Way.

"Dick problems?" Nicky inquired as Alina put her cell phone back in her purse.

"Many," she answered, playing it off.

***

E-Way showered and was soon out of the door. He drove down to the river to holler at Old Man Frank. "Do you ever go home, Pops?" he asked as he climbed aboard the yacht.

Old Man Frank was seated in his nook sipping a Mississippi Mud beer with his feet crossed at the ankles and his eyes closed. "I gotta enjoy this weather while it's here. Couple of months and I'll be stuck in the ole' house. What's up, Son. You want a beer?"

"Yeah, why not?" E-Way took a seat across from Old Man Frank.

Old Man Frank returned with a beer and the chess board. E-Way dumped the pieces our and began setting them up.

"So what's on your mind?" Old Man Fran asked as he made the first move.

"It's Skyy. I think she's cheating on me."

"That's to be expected." The old man took a swallow of his beer.

"What you mean that's to be expected?" E-Way's face was balled up.

"Focus on the game. What I mean is, only a fool would believe his woman is faithful. Let me ask you a question. Are you faithful?" He hesitated before going on. "I didn't think," he said, no longer giving E-Way a chance to answer. "So what makes you think a woman is faithful? No man could ever possibly satisfy a woman. It's impossible. A woman is too needy. She needs at least four niggas to make up that one nigga that doesn't exist. She needs a money getter, which is you. She needs an intellect, a feminine nigga who's in touch with his feelings, a family man and a host of other shit they be having on their little lists. You only fit one of the many. That's why I'm still a bachelor because I know what's in a woman's nature. If you can't deal with her cheating as you call it, then cut her ass loose." Old Man Fran lined up for his next move. "Checkmate. Ole tender dick ass nigga. That's what's wrong with you young niggas. You done convinced ya' self that you alone can satisfy a woman. Fool, don't you know that a bitch ain't never satisfied? Why ya' think a bitch can have multiple orgasms? Cause they ass ain't never gon' be satisfied."

E-Way didn't want to break things off with Skyy, but he damn sure wasn't going to sit back and do nothing while she cheated on him. The question was, what was he going to do. He drove to the hospital because it was the day that Grams was supposed to be released. He wheeled her to the car, put her in the passenger seat, and then drove her home. The doctor ordered that she stay off of her feet for at least two weeks.

Grams wasn't buying it. As soon she got home she was off to the kitchen. She had to cook something. She felt like she'd neglected the family—her oldest brother, her son, and her three great-grandchildren whom all lived with her. Grams had always put family before anything, including herself. E-Way tried to get her to do as the doctor ordered, but to no avail. Grams was a town favorite so everyone stopped by to see about her and of course to taste some of her famous home cooking.

"Matt, have you looked at any buildings for the restaurant?" Grams asked as she served dinner, literally fixing everyone's plate.

"I saw a building on Moenart and 7 Mile next to Dot and Etta's. It looks like a good location. I wrote the realtor's number down. I'm going to see what their latest request is and then make a bid."

"While I was in the hospital I made up a menu of all the dishes I would serve. My friend Ms. Mae could do the desserts and a couple of other ladies from the church can help cook and take orders." Grams was beaming.

"Sounds like a plan, Momma," E-Way said in between bites.

Grams had everything figured out to the last detail. Ma Dukes' would sure be a smash hit, but what would E-Way do? After leaving Momma's, E-Way drove out to the cemetery. He was just now accepting the fact that Bubbs had passed away. He got the plot number from Momma and told her that he was about to visit Bubbles' grave site.

E-Way walked slowly as he approached Bubbles' tombstone. He fell to his knees and started crying as he read the inscription and saw the photo on the marker. For a good while E-Way didn't say anything—he couldn't. Deep down, he felt responsible for Bubbs' death. He felt like he was supposed to be there; he was supposed to be the one laying six feet under.

"I'm sorry, Bubbs," he kept saying over and over again. "I'm sorry, Man. Man, I'm leaving the streets alone. I wish you were still here with me, my nigga…we could leave 'em together. Out of all of us, you was the only one who had a vision. I'm starting to see your vision, Bubbs, and you can live through me. The studio got burned down, but I'm a rebuild it and get things back going. Man, I miss you, my nigga. Things ain't been the same for me lately. Grams got out of the hospital. She aight though. Them clowns that did this to you…we took care of that. I just wish I had been there, Man. I'm so sorry." E-Way leaned over Bubbs' tombstone and continued to cry his eyes out.

Chapter 14

Nicky drug Skyy downtown to the Cass Corridors. It was by far one of the grimiest parts of Detroit. It was the headquarters for every heroin addict and supplier. They were on their way to visit Trina at Harbor Light halfway house. It was sponsored by the Salvation Army and Nicky had helped Trina enroll after the funeral. There she would begin her recovery.

"Why we have to come down here?" asked Skyy as she looked at all the junkies outside the building.

The parade of dope fiends were already pegging Nicky's Benz.

"For support! Now come on and remember to be nice," Nicky answered as he cut the engine.

Skyy followed Nicky up to the entrance clutching her purse with one hand inside of it on her pepper spray. They were finally buzzed in and ushered to the cafeteria where they waited for Trina. She had just finished a twelve step class when Nicky and Skyy arrived. She was told by her guidance counselor that she had some visitors. Trina entered the semi-crowded cafeteria looking like new money, wearing one of the many outfits that Nicky had bought her. When Nicky stood up to greet Trina he put his hands over his mouth in astonishment. Trina stopped and struck a pose as Skyy often did when feeling herself.

"Oh my God! Trina, you are killing that get up," Nick said as he spun Trina around. "Skyy, isn't she looking good?"

"She's looks aight," Skyy replied, trying not to give Trina too much credit. As much as Skyy hated to admit it, she really couldn't deny it. She had never in her life seen her mom look that good, except in pictures from back in the day.

"So what brings y'all down here?" Trina asked as she took a seat next to Skyy.

"We came to check up on you and make sure everything was okay. Are you alright? Do you need anything?" Nicky asked.

"Nah, I'm okay, Baby. But thank you. It's good to see you, Skyy. Thanks for coming."

"Uh-huh," Skyy mumbled.

Nicky kicked her under the table and bucked her eyes.

"So, Trina, have you been looking for employment?" Nicky asked, trying to keep the conversation going.

"Yeah, I been looking, but ain't nobody hiring no forty-five year old ex-crack head with no credentials," Trina replied. "But, I'm a keep looking."

"What are you going to do when you're released from the program?"

"I really don't know, Baby." Trina hadn't really thought that far ahead.

"Well, in the mean time you could help us out around the shop."

Skyy kicked Nicky in his shin and bucked her eyes. She nearly reached across the table to strangle him.

"What would I do?" Trina asked.

"We're always in need of an extra shampoo girl and a receptionist. What do you say?" Nicky asked.

"I don't know." Trina turned to Skyy. "What do you think, Skyy, Baby?"

Skyy balled her face up and didn't answer at first. Then, she thought about the conversation she'd had with Nicky a couple of days before. "It doesn't sound like a bad idea I guess," she heard herself say and immediately regretted coming down with Nicky.

Nicky smiled. "Well, it's settled!"

Trina was so excited that Skyy had finally let her guard down a bit. Skyy too felt a little better. Seeing Trina all dolled up and sincerely trying to change her life made her want to begin anew. They all sat around talking fashion and about Henry's Palace. Nicky had promised that he would take Trina to Henry's on her first home pass. They chatted until visiting hours ended. By that time, neither Skyy nor Trina wanted the visit to end. Skyy looked at her watch and was shocked at how much time had slipped away. They stood and said their goodbyes. Trina hugged and thanked Nicky for all that he had done and then reached over to hug Skyy. Skyy didn't refuse her, but she was stuck not knowing what to do.

"Thank you, Skyy. I hope to see you again soon," Trina said while embracing her daughter.

Skyy had to hold back the tears that formed in her eyes. Trina provided the hug that only a mother possessed. Skyy had never been hugged like that before and she felt like there was nothing in the world that could harm her at that moment. She took a deep breath and then reached up to hug

Trina back. Not wanting to seem weak by showing her emotions, Skyy quickly ended the hug.

"I'll see you later, Trina. It's good to see you doing well for yourself. Keep it up," Skyy told her mother as she and Nicky made their exit.

"I'm so proud of you for giving your mom a chance," Nicky said as he and Skyy drove on to the salon. "She really needed that."

"Yeah, well…she got one chance to fuck up and I'm done with her ass," Skyy replied. She was having mixed emotions about Trina. A part of her still wanted to hate her mother and the other part wanted to bury the hatchet.

"Girl, I saw how you were trembling when Trina hugged you. It's okay, Skyy. You can let down your guard. Remember, try and forgive her, Baby."

Skyy was hearing Nicky and wanted to forgive Trina so bad, but her heart and emotions made it hard to do so. She wanted to hate Trina for the rest of her life.

~ Chapter 15 ~

After leaving the cemetery, E-Way went to holler at Subi at the grocery store. Subi had told him to meet him there because his package was ready. E-Way strolled through the entrance of the store as usual as if he was a customer. He headed towards the meat section, stopped in front of the two stainless steel doors, and then looked around before entering. Subi was in his office on the phone delegating orders to his younger brother, Abdullah, who ran one of their car lots. Subi slammed the phone down as E-Way entered the room.

"E, Baby! What's up my nigga?" His round body rose as he grinned widely.

"Here you go with that nigga shit. You got my shit ready, Man?" E-Way asked, standing in front of Subi's desk.

"Take a seat," Subi said, motioning towards a chair. "Now, what is it that you wanted to tell me? The last time I saw you, you said we needed to talk."

"After this my good friend, I'm done."

"If it's the coke or the prices, you know I'm a fair guy. I'm willing to bend a little."

"Nah, nah. I mean, I'm done with the business altogether. It's a wrap."

"I would hate to see you go. Can I ask you why you're leaving the field?"

"It's time to do something else. I'm getting out before it's too late."

"E, it would be a slap to the face if the family were to find out that you were still in the business," Subi warned, thinking that maybe E-Way had found another supplier.

"So what the fuck? You calling me a liar?" E-Way sat up straight in his chair.

"Not at all. I'm just saying that if you wish to get back in the business, do business with those who've proved loyal. That's all."

"Yeah, whatever, Man. Where my goods at? I got shit to do." E-Way stood to his feet feeling as if Subi had threatened him on the sly before trying to clean it up while still getting his point across.

"Follow me," Subi said as he led the way down to the freezer.

He counted out fifty kilos and then handed them to E-Way to place in brown paper bags. E-Way in turn gave Subi a duffle bag full of currency.

"Remember, my boy, if you change your mind holler at me," Subi said as he let E-Way out through the back docking area.

E-Way didn't even acknowledge Subi. He loaded the kilos into the hatch of his Range Rover and then pulled out of the parking lot. He flipped open his phone and began calling all of KFB. Within minutes, everyone was pulling in front of Chuck's mother's house. They all filed into the basement and got the perspective shares.

"This is it…the last of the Mohicans," E-Way said after he finished passing out everyone's rations. He flopped down on the love seat and grabbed a Swisher Sweet off of the coffee table and began rolling a blunt.

"When you gon' turn me on to the plug?" Big Whitney asked.

Everyone's attention was on E-Way.

He hadn't prepared for the question. He licked his blunt sealed and then flicked the flame of a lighter across it to dry it.

"Well, what the plug say?" Kev inquired, growing impatient.

"He ain't trying to meet nobody," E-Way said before lighting his L and taking a long pull. *There, I said it*, he thought.

"Fuck you mean, he ain't trying to meet nobody? Like we some ole' odd ball ass niggas or something. So, what the fuck we gon' do? Are you gon' continue to cop for us?" Kev was visibly upset and wanted E-Way to shoot straight.

"If I do that I might as well stay in the game. I told y'all I'm done," E-Way said, taking another pull from his L.

"Who is the nigga?" Chuck asked.

"I can't tell you that."

"You on some ole' secret squirrel ass shit. *I can't tell you that*," Kev said, mocking E-Way.

"So basically fuck us is what you're saying?" Big Whitney asked.

"What, Nigga?" E-Way was defensive.

"I knew that nigga wasn't gon' turn us on with the plug," Kev said.

"I don't even think you hollered at the plug for real, for real," Chuckie Boms added.

Everybody was ganging up on E-Way. He couldn't believe what he was hearing. *These ungrateful ass bitches*, he thought. "I raised you niggas from a pup to a mutt, now you got fleas and wanna bite!" He stood to his feet.

"Nigga, you already rich! You got yours and now you like fuck us," Kev retorted.

"Who put two bricks in yo' hand? *I* put two bricks in all y'all hands and told y'all to blow up. It ain't my fault if you fucked over all the money you made. I'm done!" E-Way headed for the door.

"That's fucked up, E," Big Whitney said as E-Way exited the basement.

E-Way threw his hands in the air and kept it moving. The rest of KFB remained in the basement, each man feeling betrayed.

"I told y'all we should have hog-tied his ass. Either him or that bitch. He'll come off that dust for that hoe," Kev said.

"Shit, it ain't too late," Big Whitney added. He was in his feelings about E-Way not plugging him in with the connect.

***

Ole' hoe ass niggas, E-Way thought as he drove towards the Detroit River. He was steaming as he thought of Kev and the rest of his crew jumping ship on him. It was like they were only fucking with him because of the money. E-Way knew that was a lie. He had grown up with all of them; they were best friends. The money can't be that serious, he thought as he pulled up to the dock. Old Man Frank wasn't in sight as E-Way boarded the yacht. "Pops, are you here?" he called out as he turned the door handle leading to the cabin area.

Old Man Frank was lying across the sectional couch as if he was asleep. The Channel 7 News was watching him instead of the other way around. Empty beer cans lined the coffee table and the stench of weed filled the cabin. E-Way walked over to Old Man Frank and shook his leg in an attempt to wake him. Old Man Frank's leg was stiff as a board.

E-Way's stomach dropped to the pits of its depth. From having seen death in the past, E-Way knew that Old Man Frank was gone. He closed the man's eyes, which were blank, and kissed him on the forehead. "Why now, Pops?" he asked, taking a seat across from Old Man Frank. It took everything within him not to lose it. He took a labored breath and told himself that Frank had lived a full life. "I did it, Pops. I'm done with the game. As you say, checkmate. You were right as always. Niggas always think you owe 'em something. I kinda fell out with my guys about not plugging them. Oh well…What am I going to do without you, Pops? First Bubbs, now you. You was like my dad, Man. You raised me from a youngin' and I thank you for all that you've done. If it wasn't for you schooling me I would have been dead a long time ago. I just wish you could see me get out the game and be a success at something else. Damn, Pops." E-Way put his hands on his face, trying to hold back the tears.

It was Old Man Frank's time to go. He was old as dirt and had done everything under the sun at least twice. He had lived his life—a long one. E-Way knew it was his time, he just didn't want to accept it. He needed Old Man Frank. But, that's life; you gain one thing and lose two. E-Way walked out onto the deck to grab a beer and then went back inside of the cabin. He continued to talk to Old Man Frank. As he looked over the man's lifeless body, he told himself that this was how he wanted to die—at peace.

~ Chapter 16 ~

Since seeing Trina, Skyy couldn't stop thinking about seeing her again so that she could ask her all of the questions that had been bothering her for so long. Skyy sat in her office in front of the computer lost in thought, day dreaming about the past and the future. Her thoughts were interrupted by the ringing of her cell phone. The call came in as unavailable so she was hesitant about answering, but reluctantly she did. "Hello?"

"Skyy, Baby how are you?" Trina asked.

Skyy was caught off guard. She recognized the voice but wondered how she'd gotten her cell number. *That damn Nicky*, Skyy thought. "I'm alright," she answered, not really knowing what to say.

"I hope I didn't catch you at a bad time.'

"Nah, it's okay. What's up?"

"Well, my guidance counselor is giving me a four-hour furlough so I can get my birth certificate and social security card. I have to get those in order to obtain my driver's license."

"You don't already have those?"

"Nope. I haven't had a copy of my birth certificate in probably twenty years and I have never had my license. I was hoping you could take me…if you're not too busy."

Shit, the bus is running, Skyy thought. "I guess I can take you. When does your furlough start?"

"Just as soon as you can get here. My time starts from the moment I sign the log book."

"Give me about twenty minutes."

"Thank you so much, Skyy."

"Uh-huh," Skyy muttered before hanging up the phone.

"Where you off to, Ms. Thang?" Nicky asked as Skyy headed for the door.

"Thanks to you Trina has my cell number. She called and asked me to play taxi for the day so she can get her license."

"I'm so proud of you. Let me know how things go, alright."

Skyy just rolled her eyes and stormed out of the shop like a spoiled brat. As she pulled in front of the dilapidated half-way house, Skyy started regretting agreeing to drive Trina around. Dope fiends decorated the exterior of the building. They leaned forward in an attempt to see who was pushing the shiny BMW. Skyy tucked her purse underneath her seat and removed her Mace before exiting the car.

"Say, Red! Can you spare a few dollars?" asked one of the many, musty fiends as Skyy headed for the entrance.

She didn't even bother answering. She knew better than to engage in a conversation and risk the chance of being robbed. The desk guard buzzed her in and handed her a log to sign. After signing in, the guard continued to eat his lunch of Popeye's Chicken. Skyy just stood in the small lobby for a few minutes growing impatient.

"Tah!" she sucked her teeth loudly. "Aren't you going to let them know I'm down here waiting?" she snapped.

The guard smacked his chops and then licked his fingers before picking up his desk phone. "And who is it that you're here to see?" he asked.

"Trina Tobias," Skyy replied with an attitude.

"She'll be down in a minute," the guard informed after hanging up the phone. He went back to attacking his lunch.

Skyy mean-mugged his fat ass while she waited.

Within minutes Trina emerged looking like a beach bunny, wearing a shorts set that Nicky had bought for her. "He ain't giving you a hard time is he?" Trina asked, referring to the guard.

"Not as hard a time as he's giving that damn chicken," Skyy answered.

"You's a mess, Girl. You better be nice to my daughter, Marion," Trina warned the guard.

"That's your daughter?" he asked. "Damn, y'all look like twins."

"You ready, Trina?" Skyy asked. She wasn't trying to hear nothing about how much she and Trina resembled.

"Yeah. I'll see you in a few, Marion," Trina said as she and Skyy made their exit. "His fat ass is always trying to holla. I'll be nice because he's in charge of the log. He can easily make my furlough for ten hours if he wanted to. Is this your car, Baby? This damn thing is sharp," Trina said as they approached the BMW.

"Yeah," Skyy answered as she rushed to unlock the doors.

Trina rubbed the dashboard and the butter soft interior in approval. "Just like yo' momma. You got expensive taste." Trina tried to get settled in her seat.

There was an awkward silence. Skyy didn't know what to say so she just focused on not being rude. Once out of the Cass Corridors, Skyy let the top down. She needed the breeze to lighten the mood a little.

Trina watched in amazement as the hardtop folded back and disappeared into the trunk. "So, Skyy…when's the last time you visited Momma?" she asked, trying to spark up some meaningful conversation.

"It's been a while. I really need to go and see her and put some flowers on her grave."

"Maybe one day soon we'll be able to do that together. I haven't visited my mom's grave in God knows how long."

"I'd like that. So, how're your treatment classes coming along?" Skyy asked, trying to change the touchy subject about her grandmother.

"I have two more weeks until graduation. Let me tell you, I haven't felt this good about myself in years. My guidance counselor wanted me to take a job as an assistant, but I told her about me working at the shop. She's all for it. She says it'll give us a chance to build up our relationship. I've got so much to learn about you, Skyy. I know I wasn't there for you growing up, but I don't want to miss another day of your life. I'm not going to pretend like the past isn't real and not acknowledge it, but Baby, it is what it is…the past. I want you to know that I'm proud of you, Skyy, for what it's worth.

You've made something of yourself and you're going places. Do you think we can start over?" Trina asked.

Skyy was caught off guard. Trina had just spilled her guts out of nowhere as if she'd been thinking about these things for a long time. Trina waited patiently for Skyy to respond.

"Let me ask you a question," Skyy said softly.

"Anything." Trina turned to face Skyy completely.

"What made you leave me? I mean, was the streets that much more important than me? Do you know all I've been through growing up without you? Do you know how many times I was raped as a child, thinking that it was normal, all the things I was subjected to? Do you know how many nights I went to bed hungry and cold? Do you have any idea?" Skyy began to cry.

Trina looked at Skyy and felt helpless. She wanted to comfort Skyy but didn't know how. All she could offer was, "Baby, I'm so sorry I left you?"

"Why'd you do it?" Skyy asked again. "Why'd you leave me?"

"I was a foolish little girl when I had you. I wasn't ready to be a mother. I was afraid that I would fail you. Baby, please forgive me. I didn't know you'd been through all those horrible things," Trina said as she too started crying. She grabbed Skyy's hand and kissed it. "Baby, you remind me of myself in more than one way. I was raped and abandoned as a child too. To hear you say that you were raped and went to bed hungry brings back ill memories. I never meant for you to go through what I did."

"How do I know you won't up and leave me again? How do I know you're really done using drugs and running the streets?"

"Baby, I assure you that my intentions are good. It's a daily battle and we can only take it one day at a time. I need you now more than ever. Don't be like me, Skyy, and turn your back on me. You're better than me and I really need your support."

Skyy pulled up in front of the Social Security Office and parked. She and Trina looked in their respective visor mirrors to gather their pretty.

"You coming in?" Trina asked.

"Nah, I'm a wait in the car. I need a moment," Skyy told her.

"Aight. I'll be just one moment." Trina exited the car and entered the building.

Skyy felt a hell of a lot better after venting her emotions. She didn't quite get the answers she was looking for out of Trina. In fact, she felt guilty for some reason. She didn't know about Trina's upbringing or of her being raped and abused as a child. Skyy tried to sympathize with Trina's situation and her reasons for leaving her only child behind. Skyy was deep in thought by the time Trina opened the passenger door and got back in the car.

"Are you okay?" Trina asked. "You look like you were in outta space."

"Yeah. I was just thinking, that's all."

"Well, one more stop. Get this damn birth certificate and next week I'll apply for my license. I may have to borrow your car for my driver's test."

"We'll see," Skyy said, pulling away from the curb.

After leaving the county's vital records office, Skyy dropped Trina back off at the halfway house. The sun was beginning to set and she wanted to get as far away as possible from the Cass Corridors before dark fell. Trina made small talk once they pulled in front of Harbor Light.

"So, are you coming to my graduation?" Trina asked.

"I'll be there along with Nicky of course," Skyy assured her.

"Thank you for everything, Skyy. Let me get in here before these folks go to tripping. I'll call you later to see if you made it in safely."

"Aight. See you later, Trina," Skyy said as she watched Trina enter the door before pulling away from the curb.

***

It was ladies night out and Skyy needed to see Chris. She met Nicky and Marie at Henry's. Also in attendance was none other than Alina's hating ass. She was there for one reason and one reason only—to bust Skyy by all means.

~ Chapter 17 ~

"Hello?" E-Way answered his phone. He was in the middle of closing the deal on the building for the restaurant.

"I've got something for you," the voice on the other end advised.

"Who is this?"

"You got that many hoes? It's Alina."

"Oh, what's up? What you got for me?"

"I'd rather show you in person. Where are you?"

"It'll have to be tomorrow or something. I'm in the middle of something right now. Just tell me what it is."

"It can wait," Alina said with an attitude.

"Aight then. I'm a hit you up later."

Alina hung up without saying bye. She was salty because E-Way didn't drop what he was doing to see what she had for him.

E-Way and his attorney finished signing all of the necessary documents. He handed the realtor a check and in return the realtor handed him the keys to the building. He stood in the dusty, unlit building smiling as he envisioned customers coming and going. After leaving the building, E-Way went to break the news to Grams. She had some news of her own to break to him as she handed him a large manila envelope the moment he entered the house. The envelope was addressed to him from a law firm.

E-Way looked down at the envelope in confusion. "What's this?" he asked.

"I don't know, Baby. The mailman dropped it off earlier. It seems very important. Open it," Grams urged as she and E-Way walked over to the sofa to take a seat.

E-Way read the contents of the letter inside in disbelief. His eyes raced through the sentences.

Grams could tell that it was something exclusive by E-Ways body language. "What is it, Baby?"

"It's Old Man Frank's will. He named me as the beneficiary to all his assets," E-Way said, handing Grams the copy of the will. E-Way stood up and began pacing the living room floor. Old Man Frank had left him twelve million cash, several rental properties, his yacht, and his estate. E-Way knew that Old Man Frank had money, but he'd never put an exact price on it.

"Baby, what are you going to do with all this money?" Grams asked.

"For starters, I'm a send Pops out in style," E-Way replied. He handed Grams the keys and the deed to the building he'd just purchased.

Her face lit up as she read over the deed. She gave E-Way a big hug and a kiss on the forehead. "Let me go call Ms. Mae!" She ran into the kitchen and grabbed the phone.

E-Way smiled to himself at the sight of Grams so happy. His smile turned to a frown at the thought of Old Man Frank passing. He grabbed the will off of the coffee table and left out of the front door. It was ten o'clock in the morning yet E-Way wanted to share the good news with Skyy, so he drove up to the salon. He was mean-mugged by Alina as he entered the shop.

Nicky noticed the eye contact between the two and commanded their attention. "*Skyy's* in the back," he announced, emphasizing Skyy's name.

"Thank you, Nicholas," E-Way said, trying to be funny as he headed towards the backroom.

Skyy was at the computer and on the phone talking to Chris when E-Way walked into the room. Her stomach dropped at the sight of him. She quickly ended her conversation. "Let me call you back," she said, hanging up on Chris without giving him an opportunity to say goodbye. "Baby, what are you doing here?" she asked E-Way as she jumped to her feet. Her palms were sweaty and she turned pale as if she'd seen a ghost.

"I came to check on you. I don't need no invitation for that, do I?" E-Way asked as he gave Skyy a kiss.

"Of course not. I'm just surprised to see you, that's all. What's this?" She pointed at the manila envelope in his hand.

"You might want to take a seat for this," he told her as he handed her the will.

Skyy opened the envelope and began reading the documentation. She stopped at the part about the twelve million. She immediately jumped into E-Ways arms excitedly. "Oh my God! Did you call these people yet?"

"Nah, I just got it a few minutes ago. I'm do that in a little while. I got some other good news. I just closed on the building for the restaurant. Everything's coming together."

"I can't believe Old Man Frank left you everything. He didn't have a family?"

"I was the only family he had…"

Chapter 18

E-Way hadn't seen or heard from Kev, Chuck, Big Whitney, or Chuckie Boms since they'd fallen out. He wasn't surprised to see them in attendance at Old Man Frank's funeral. Damn near the entire east side of Detroit packed the pews of Word of Faith Church. Those who weren't on the approved list of guests watched the service from a monitor posted outside of the church. Old Man Frank was a legend. People from all over came to show their support.

E-Way and Skyy sat in the front pew; they were deemed as Old Man Frank's family. Alongside them were all of Old Man Frank's young skeezers whom he sponsored and laid up with from time to time. They were all hoping to be named in the man's will. Little did they know, E-Way had already collected all that would be issued from Old Man Frank's estate. E-Way looked at each of them with his face screwed up. *Shysty ass bitches*, he thought.

Several people gave eulogies about Old Man Frank—how they'd met him and what a good-hearted man he was. E-Way didn't give a eulogy. He wanted the services to end as soon as possible. He felt like for the most part everyone there had a hidden agenda with the exception of a few people. E-Way thought, *Old Man Frank didn't even fuck with these niggas like that.* After the services everyone tailed Old Man Frank's hearse to the burial site and then everyone met at the State Fair Lounge for the repast.

E-Way was rather reserved. He and Skyy sat tucked off in a corner sipping Remy Martin VSOP. Everyone knew how close Old Man Frank was to E-Way so they stopped by his table to give their sympathy and condolences. Kev and the rest of KFB approached E-Way and Skyy's table.

E-Way told Skyy to excuse herself so that he could holler at his men for a second. He was hoping they wouldn't be disrespectful and bring up the connect situation.

"I'll be over here if you need me, Baby," Skyy said, kissing E-Way on the cheek before getting up.

The crew all took seats facing E-Way who still hadn't said a word to any of them.

"E, Man...I'm sorry about Old Man Frank," Big Whitney said breaking the ice. "I know how close y'all were."

Everyone else offered their sympathy as well.

"Thank y'all for coming, Man. What y'all niggas been up to?" E-Way asked.

"Same ole' two step for real. Niggas trying to find a connect with some decent prices."

E-Way tolerated the conversation because he missed his niggas, but he wasn't trying to hear nothing about no drugs. His mind was on higher stakes and he just wished that his crew would see his vision and dare to dream big outside of the streets. Here it was that Old Man Frank was dead and E-Way was mourning, yet all these niggas could think about was themselves. They kept hinting about getting plugged. E-Way felt as though that was the only reason they were there.

Mario, the music producer who was also the guy that Skyy had run into at the salon and the after party, approached E-Way's table. He too had known Old Man Frank before making it big in the music industry. Mario used to promote events which sparked his relationship with Old Man Frank. He used to promote gatherings at Frank's bar and other star-studded events.

"E-Way, Man, I'm sorry about the loss of Frank. If there's anything I can do, Man, don't hesitate to ask," Mario told E-Way.

"I'm good, Man, but thanks anyway," E-Way replied.

"I see you got your crew with you. I ain't heard nothing from y'all lately. What, y'all not rapping no more?"

The question hadn't really been pondered since the death of Bubbles.

"Yeah, we still doing us. I'm about to rebuild the bar and studio. Just with the loss of Bubbs, shit got kinda stagnant," E-Way answered.

"I still want to do something y'all, Man. Y'all definitely got what it takes. Whenever y'all ready let me know."

"I'm a get up with you."

"Aight. Y'all be smooth," Mario said as he excused himself.

"Man, fuck that fake ass Berry Gordy ass nigga. I'm trying to get this paper how I know how. Later for the rap shit," Kev said as Mario left the table.

"Man, I'm getting ready to get up out of here. Y'all niggas get up with me, Man." E-Way stood to his feet. He couldn't stand being there a moment longer.

All of them looked like they wanted to ask him about the connect but they didn't.

"Aight, we'll get up with you probably tomorrow or something," Big Whitney said.

E-Way thanked everyone for coming as he and Skyy exited the lounge.

"Come on. Let's get the fuck up outta here," Kev suggested.

***

The next day Trina graduated from her twelve-step program. Skyy took E-Way and Nicky along to show Trina some support. It was set up like an actual graduation, minus the caps and gowns. Trina opened up the ceremony with a song by Whitney Houston; she sang it as if she'd wrote it. Skyy watched in amazement. She had no idea that Trina could blow like that. E-Way was ever more blown away by Trina's performance. He felt that he'd just found his first artist as everyone stood giving Trina a standing ovation.

"Trina, I didn't know you had vocal skills like that," Skyy said excitedly as she met Trina at the end of the stage.

"Have you ever thought about recording anything?" E-Way asked.

"Not really," Trina answered honestly.

"Well listen, I would like to sign you to a recording contract. With your voice and image you're guaranteed to sell. You've got a story to tell," E-Way encouraged her.

"You sound pretty convicted," Trina remarked.

"Just give it a chance. What do you have to lose?"

"Go for it, Trina," Nicky said.

"Yeah, Ma…I mean, Trina," Skyy added, catching herself.

Trina smiled at the thought of Skyy calling her Ma. "Let's do it," she said.

~ Chapter 19 ~

E-Way couldn't sleep. He just knew that he'd discovered the next big thing in R&B. He called Mario and told him about Trina. Mario told him to bring her by the studio so that she could put together a demo of about five songs. Trina was now living with Skyy and E-Way until she was stable enough to get her own spot. E-Way interrupted Skyy and Trina's conversation as they were seated in the kitchen looking at some furniture for their new house. Skyy and E-Way were moving into Old Man Frank's estate after everything was settled.

"I hate to break up y'all Martha Stewart home shopping network session and what not, but Trina I need for you to throw something on and take a ride with me," E-Way said.

"Where you taking her this early in the morning?" Skyy asked, looking up from the catalog.

"To the studio. Mario wants her to put together a demo."

"Who you think you is, Puffy or Jermaine Dupri or something?" Skyy joked.

"What time do we have to be there?" Trina asked.

"As soon as possible," E-Way answered, looking at his watch and then clapping his hands together. "Let's go, let's go," he said, like a professional manager.

"Can I come?" Skyy asked.

"Yeah, but don't be all in the way."

Trina recorded five songs that Mario had written. He only had to run the melody of each song one time along with the instrumental for Trina. After playing the tracks, Mario sat at the mixing board counting the perspective figures he was about to pocket. There was no doubt in is mind that Trina was a born, undiscovered star. The demo came out better than he'd expected. Skyy, E-Way, Mario, and a few other industry folks filled the studio. They all gave Trina kudos as she exited the sound booth. Mario as trying to sign her to his record label.

"Slow down there, Suge Knight," E-Way cut in. "She's signed to me. I just wanted you to produce her."

"Fifty-fifty split," Mario said.

"I said produce, not rape!"

"Sixty-forty."

E-Way shook his head.

"Seventy-thirty, my final offer."

"Deal," E-Way said, extending his hand. He and Mario made a verbal agreement sealed by their handshake.

"I'll have my lawyer draw the papers up. Baby, you're about to be a star," Mario insisted, smiling at Trina who was soaking up every moment of the attention.

"I'm a be your stylist," Skyy said. "Can't have you out here looking skeptical."

Trina was overwhelmed. She didn't care one way or the other; as long as Skyy was happy, she was content.

After leaving the studio, Skyy took Trina out to celebrate and what better place to do so than at Henry's Palace? Skyy called Nicky and told him to meet them there. It was early in the day so the bar was rather naked so far as customers go. Skyy, Nicky, and Trina didn't mind because that meant more dick for them. Trina grinned from ear to ear at all of the young stallions as they took to the stage doing their sets.

"So this is Henry's Palace?" Trina asked as she looked around. "How long has this place been here?"

"Not long enough," Nicky replied.

"Skyy, who are you looking for? You keep turning around as if someone is following us," Trina commented.

"She waiting on her thang-thang Chris," Nicky said, teasing Skyy.

"Who is Chris?" Trina asked.

"Just the finest nigga to ever walk the face of this earth. I wonder why he isn't here." Skyy continued to scan the bar in search of Chris.

"You better be careful not to get caught up with this Chris, Baby," Trina warned.

"I keep telling her," Nicky stated.

Skyy wasn't hearing them. She grabbed her cell phone and called Chris to see where he was.

Chris was pulling into the parking lot of Henry's Palace as his cell rang. Skyy met him at the entrance of the bar as if they were a serious couple. Nicky pointed in Chris' direction, showing Trina who it was that Skyy was tripping off.

"Bae is fine," Trina said in approval as Skyy and Chris approached the table.

Skyy introduced Chris to Trina.

Chris couldn't believe that Trina was Skyy's mother. "This is your mom?" he asked.

"Chico DeBarge, when are you going on stage?" Nicky joked.

"I don't go on until late night. You know I'm like a headliner. They always save the best for last," Chris shot back.

"Well, can I get an exclusive show?" Skyy asked, rubbing on Chris' stomach.

"Come on, follow me. It was nice meeting you, Ma'am," Chris said as he led Skyy towards the rear of the bar.

She looked back at Nicky and Trina smiling as she trailed Chris.

"Details!" Nicky yelled.

***

E-Way met Alina in downtown Detroit at the Marriot Hotel. He had booked a room and was upstairs waiting on her. He left a key at the front desk for Alina to retrieve upon arriving. Alina entered the room to find E-Way lying across the sofa in the living room area. She was still acting stank because E-Way hadn't dropped what he was doing the last time they spoke so that he could see what she had for him. E-Way got up and attempted to touch Alina but she jerked away.

"If I would have known you were gon' be acting shifty I would've stayed home," he told her.

"Whatever. Here," Alina said, handing E-Way her cell phone.

E-Way looked at the phone confusedly. "Why you giving me this?"

"There's some pictures on there."

E-Way scrolled through several photos of Skyy hugged up with Chris at Henry's. He was unfazed until he stopped at the last photo. It was a picture of Skyy kissing Chris goodbye in the parking lot. Chris was gripping Skyy's ass with a yard of tongue down her throat. E-Way turned the cell phone off and asked, "Can I keep this?"

"For how long?"

"I'll bring it right back," E-Way said, heading for the door.

"Where are you going?" Alina asked.

"I'm a call you," E-Way said as he exited the room leaving Alina standing there looking and feeling stupid.

E-Way wasn't in the mood for what Alina had in mind. She thought that after she gave him the pictures that he would leave Skyy. Alina stood in the hotel room feeling used as E-Way left the hotel and drove straight to Henry's Palace. He wanted to holler at Chris and see just how involved he was with Skyy. E-Way noticed Skyy's BMW parked in the lot as he pulled in. Parked next to her car was Nicky's Benz.

E-Way valet parked his truck and then entered the bar. He noticed Nicky and Trina seated center stage, both receiving lap dances. E-Way stormed towards their table and Nicky's eyes bucked at the sight of him.

"Where Skyy at?" E-Way demanded.

"E-Way, what are you doing here?" Nicky asked.

Skyy and Chris came walking up flirting. Skyy stopped dead in her tracks as she met eyes with E-Way. Nicky, Trina, Skyy, and Chris all looked as if they'd seen a ghost.

"This how you gon' play me?" E-Way asked.

"Baby, I told you we just come here for leisure," Skyy tried to explain.

"You just gon' go to the grave with yo' shit, huh?" E-Way asked, tossing Skyy Alina's cell phone and walking out.

Skyy wanted to go after E-Way but she knew not to or else she'd risk the chance of a beat down.

"That's yo' nigga?" Chris asked as he watched E-way leave out.

Skyy stood there dumbfounded. She didn't know what to do.

"Girl, you better go after him," Trina advised.

"Yeah, you should go see about your man," Chris suggested sarcastically.

By the time Skyy made it out to the parking lot E-Way was already in traffic. She tried calling is cell, but E-Way kept pushing the END button.

What the hell he give me this phone for, Skyy wondered as she walked back inside of the bar. She started scrolling through the phone and discovered that it belonged to Alina. "What the fuck he doing with Alina's phone?" she asked as she handed the cell to Nicky for his inspection.

"Look at this, Skyy," Nicky said, showing Skyy the pictures of her and Chris.

"I'm a kill that bitch," Skyy said.

~ Chapter 20 ~

Skyy stayed out as late as possible. She dreaded going home and having to face E-Way. Trina tried coaching her, telling her to be honest and let the chips fall where they may. Skyy trembled as she stuck her house key in the lock and turned the knob.

"I'll be downstairs if you need me," Trina said before heading to her room in the basement.

Skyy found E-Way in their bedroom watching T.V. He laid on the bed staring at the screen but not comprehending what he was watching. Skyy entered the room without saying a word. She walked over to the chair at her vanity table and took a seat. E-Way hadn't acknowledged her presence. He just continued to stare out of space. There was no sense in trying to carry on a lie. It was over; E-Way had busted her.

"E-Way, can we talk, Baby?" she asked.

"What is there to talk about? It is what it is. You been lying to me all this time. Sucking that nigga's dick and then coming home and kissing me like nothing happened."

"I don't love him, I love you."

"And that's supposed to make everything alright? *You don't love him*," E-Way repeated.

"What about you? How did you get Alina's cell phone?"

"Like I said, it is what it is. You was doing you and I was doing me. We was both living a lie."

"So…what now?" Skyy asked.

"Ain't no sense in stopping now. Continue to do you. I'm not saying that I'm done fucking with you or that I don't love you anymore, because I do. It's just hard to stomach. To be honest, I don't know where we'll go from here."

Skyy didn't say anything because there was really nothing that could be said. They both knew about their infidelities. They both knew that the other was doing their own thing on the side, but now that it was out in the open it seemed as if they couldn't move on. Skyy crawled in bed next to E-Way with her back to him. She was thinking about how badly she wished that she'd never gotten caught up with Chris. E-Way was reflecting on what Old Man Frank had told him about women and it being in their nature to cheat.

The next morning Skyy awoke lying next to E-Way. They had both slept in their clothes. E-Way was still sound asleep. Skyy pulled his shoes off and then covered him with the comforter. She kissed his forehead and then headed towards the bathroom to get ready for another day at the shop.

"How did things go last night, Baby?" Trina asked as Skyy entered the kitchen. Trina was seated at the counter drinking tea and doing a crossword puzzle.

"I really don't know. I think he understood for the most part. He didn't give me the feeling it was over. What I got is out of it is that we have an unspoken agreement for each of us to do our thing but consider the other person's feelings."

"That reminds me of me and your father's early relationship. After so long that's just how it is. That doesn't mean you lose love for the person you're with. It's hard to explain, but trust and believe I know where you're coming from."

Skyy said goodbye to Trina and was off to the shop. She wore a pair of sweats, some Air Force Ones, and a t-shirt. She had her hair pulled back into a ponytail and she was ready. She entered the shop and all eyes turned towards her. Nicky was doing a customer's head. He hadn't said a word to Alina about what she had done. Nicky wanted to let Skyy handle the situation. All morning however, Alina had been acting shifty. She knew that ass was hit from the look in Skyy's eyes as she stopped in front of her chair.

"I need to see you in the back, Alina," Skyy said.

"As soon as I finish with this head," Alina said nervously.

"Now!" Skyy yelled as she started for the back.

Alina excused herself from her customer. She grabbed her purse and bolted for the front door, but Nicky jumped in front of her and pointed towards the backroom. Everyone in the shop was looking and wondering what the hell was going on. No one knew about Alina's episode with E-Way and her taking pictures of Skyy and Chris.

"Nicky, please let me explain," Alina pleaded.

"You's the worst kind of bitch…a jealous bitch," Nicky told her.

Skyy returned to the front of the shop. She grabbed Alina by the hair and drug her into the back.

"Beat that bitch ass!" Erica instigated the matter. "I never liked that creepy bitch no way."

Tae played peacemaker and pulled Skyy off of Alina, holding Skyy back until Alina could make a safe exit.

"Don't come back, Bitch!" Nicky said as Alina hightailed it out of the shop with a well whooped ass.

Skyy had pulled a plug of hair from Alina's scalp and busted her nose. She didn't get her how she wanted to though. If it wasn't for Tae, Alina would have gotten a far worse ass whopping. The only reason that Skyy stopped was because of the respect that she had for Tae.

After the shop settled down, Skyy sat at her desk thinking about Chris. She wanted to dismiss him, but was too far gone to do so. After being busted it just felt wrong all of a sudden. Skyy decided to fall back on Chris for as long as she could and deal with him on an as-needed basis which would be whenever she needed to release some stress or just be able to go somewhere outside of the norm and let her hair down. This was her way of rationalizing the situation.

***

Meanwhile, E-Way met with Old Man Frank's attorney so that the deceased man's will could be released. His attorney handed E-Way the keys to Old Man Frank's estate, all the deeds to the investment properties, and then completed a wire transfer for the twelve million dollars from Frank's account to E-Way's bank. E-Way left the attorney's office feeling like a new man. With twelve million behind him he could damn near do anything business-wise. On his way back into the city he stopped at an exotic car lot.

A four door cocaine white Bentley caught his eye. It was parked on the showroom floor.

E-Way went almost unnoticed as he entered the dealership. The salesman didn't bother approaching him because he didn't come off as the type to possess the $320,000.00 listed on the bill of sale in the window of the Bentley that E-Way was gawking at. E-Way tried the driver's side door in an attempt to get in, but the doors were locked. He looked around and then motioned to a salesman. The sales rep reluctantly came over. He was a middle-aged white man with salt and pepper hair; very clean cut. He wore an Italian cut blue power suit and Italian cut loafers.

"How may I assist you, Sir?" the salesman asked.

"I want to test drive this," E-Way said.

The man laughed silently with his mouth open as he looked up at the ceiling. "I'm sorry, Sir, but we don't usually test drive here. Our customers usually buy the cars first. They've been driving that particular brand for a while and know what to expect." He was attempting to shoot E-Way down.

"Well, *Sir,*" E-Way said, mocking the sales rep. "Before I spend $320,000.00 I would like to test drive this damn car. I don't care to hear what you usually do. Where's the manager?"

Again the man silently laughed, looked up at the ceiling, and then shot back at E-Way. "We don't carry the term *manager* here, Sir. We are all co-owners." He pointed around at the assorted white faces. "However, if you insist on test driving I will draw the keys, but we must first check your credentials."

"Credentials?" E-Way repeated.

"Yes. Bank accounts, stocks, bonds, etcetera. We must, it's protocol."

E-Way reached into his pocket and handed the man a piece of paper with his account number on it, the same account that Old Man Frank's attorney had just wired his inheritance to. E-Way then handed over his driver's license.

"Very well. I will be right back," the man said, leaving E-Way to finish dreaming about the Bentley. The sales rep walked over to his office and typed the account number into his computer. His eyes bucked at the dollars indicated on the screen. He looked out of the window at E-Way and then back at the computer screen. He tapped the monitor and then sprinted out of the office grabbing the keys. His entire attitude had changed. "If you don't like this color we can order whatever color you desire. The same applies to the interior and rims," he informed as he handed E-Way the keys and they set off for a quick test drive.

"Nah, I'll take this one," E-Way said as they pulled back into the dealership.

"Excellent choice. Just let me draw up the papers and I can have you on your way," the rep said, racing back to his office.

After all of the paper work was handled, E-Way was allowed to drive off in his shiny new Bentley. His truck was to be delivered to his house by a towing service courtesy of the dealership. E-Way called Kev to see where everybody was. He wanted to stunt and show off his Bentley. All of KFB was at Chuck's momma's house in the basement smoking blunts and playing Play Station 2. E-Way called inside once he pulled in front of the house and told everyone to come outside.

"Who the fuck this nigga think he is?" Kev asked, hanging up the phone.

"Who is that?" Chuck asked.

"E-Way. He talking about all us come outside."

"He in front of the house?" Big Whit asked.

"I guess."

They all got up and headed outside through the side door. E-Way had all of the windows down so that his sounds could be heard. He was leaning up against the car with his arms folded like a boss when the crew walked up. They all looked at the car in awe.

"This how you doing it now?" Chuck asked.

"Ah you know, nigga gotta treat his self every now and again," E-Way said, going into boss mode.

"Let me take this mothafucka around the corner," Big Whitney said.

"Shit, let's ride out."

"I gotta handled some business. I'm gon' get with y'all niggas later," Chuck said.

"Aight then," E-Way replied as he, Kev, Big Whit, and Chuckie Boms piled into the Bentley.

Big Whitney drove while E-Way rode shotgun. Kev and Chuckie Boms were seated in the back.

"It's enough wood in this bitch to start a fire," Kev said as he climbed in.

"Roll up the windows so we can catch a cloud," Chuckie Boms requested.

They rode downtown to Belle Isle, circling the island three times before leaving. They parlayed at River Rouge Park and then Chandler Park. By the time the sun went down they had been through every part of Detroit from east to west and back. Not wanting the night to end, Big Whitney suggested that they hit a strip club called Pretty Woman. They pulled up like bosses, valet parked the car, and entered the club like hood stars. E-Way paid for a booth in V.I.P. and within minutes they were swarmed by a pack of young ladies offering lap dances.

"Bar on me tonight," E-Way said, informing the shot girl.

"Damn, Big Timer. What you do, sign with Cash Money Records?" Big Whit asked.

"Yeah, you round here pulling up in Bentleys and buying out the bar. What's good?" Kev asked.

E-Way hadn't told them about Old Man Frank leaving him a fortune nor did he have any plans on telling them. Kev, Chuckie Boms, and Big Whitney were left to assume that what they had already expected—that E-Way had gotten right and said fuck them. Their imaginations were getting the best of them. *That's what happens when niggas start trying to count your money*, E-Way thought.

"Y'all niggas worried about the wrong thing," E-Way told them as he enjoyed the lap dance from two dancers.

Kev couldn't even enjoy himself. He was too focused on E-Way. From the corner of the booth he mean-mugged E-Way as he plotted on his downfall. It was like the two young ladies who were draped over him didn't exist. Chuckie Boms and Big Whitney were in a similar mood. E-Way excused himself to uses the bathroom. After he left the booth, Kev leaned over and to Big Whitney who was seated next to him.

"Man, we gon' do that shit tonight," Kev decided.

"Tonight?" Big Whitney was skeptical.

"Tonight! Soon as we leave this bitch."

Chapter 21

E-Way returned to the booth where Kev, Chuckie Boms, and Big Whitney were seated. They continued to pop bottles and enjoy lap dances until the club closed. E-Way paid the bar tab and exchanged numbers with one of the dancers promising to get up with her in the near future. He was buzzing good from all of the bubbly and shots of liquor. He exited the bar to find Big Whitney, Kev, and Chuckie Boms already in the car. He walked around to the passenger side and got in after hollering at a few groupies in the parking lot. Big Whitney pulled out of the parking lot and turned onto a side street leading back to the hood. It was just past two o'clock in the morning; they had been hanging since early in the afternoon and E-Way was ready to call it a night.

He flipped open his cell phone and scrolled down to Skyy's name. As the phone began ringing, Chuckie Boms, who was seated behind E-Way, reached forward and choked E-Way from behind. He had him in a Full-Nelson wrestling move, cutting off E-Way's windpipe. Big Whitney reached over from the driver's seat and frisked E-Way's waistband, removing his pistol. E-Way tussled as much as he could, but was caught off guard. He tried to slide down in his seat so that he could come out of Chuckie Boms' chokehold, but it was useless.

"Why y'all doing this?" E-Way managed to ask. His life was flashing before his eyes. The lack of oxygen caused him to pass out. His body went limp as he slumped over and ceased in resistance.

"Hello? E-Way? Baby, are you okay?" Skyy asked into the phone.

E-Way's cell was still on as it lay on the floor between his legs.

Big Whitney reached down between E-Way's legs and grabbed the cell phone.

"Hello? Hello?" Skyy called out over and over until the phone went dead.

Big Whitney hung up on her and then turned the phone completely off. They pulled in front of Chuck's mother's house where all of their cars were parked. Kev sprinted inside to grab Chuck and some rope so they could tie E-Way up. Kev and Chuck returned to the car carrying a large brown box and an industrial size extension cord instead of the rope.

E-Way began to regain his senses but was still dazed and unable to move. Kev opened the passenger door and snatched E-Way out onto the curb. The street was completely dark; no one was out at this hour. E-Way was left to fend for himself. His only prayer in the world was that a police car would just so happen to ride past and save him. He knew that the odds of that were slim to none because of the street lights being shot out and the recent violence against police.

Kev and Big Whitney rolled E-Way over onto his back and began tying him up with the extension cord. E-Way laid there with his eyes open staring at the stars. He couldn't believe what was taking place. All he could think about was what Old Man Frank had told him. *Death is near* and *them niggas gon' be the death of you.*

"This how y'all gon' do me?" E-Way asked.

"Nigga, we gon' give yo' bitch ass one chance and one chance only to make a call and get some money. We tired of playing with yo' ass," Kev said as he finished tying E-Way.

What the fuck is he talking about, being tired of playing with me, E-Way wondered. He grew angry at the thought.

"So, it was y'all who broke into my house?" he asked.

No one said anything. It was all starting to make sense. No wonder nothing had been taken.

"You bitch made ass niggas. Which one of you niggas put y'all hands on my grandmother?" E-Way yelled as he tried to sit up but was unable.

"As much as we'd love to take a trip down memory lane with you, we can't. What you gon' do?" Kev asked, looking down at E-Way.

Big Whitney called Skyy back using E-Way's cell phone. Once Skyy answered Big Whitney bent down and put the phone to E-Way's ear.

"Hello?" Skyy called out.

"Man, tell her to put together a million dollars and have it ready immediately," Big Whitney instructed while holding the phone to E-Way's ear.

"E-Way, are you there?" Skyy asked.

"Baby, listen…I love you. I just want you to know that."

"What's wrong, Baby?" Skyy asked, sensing that something was wrong with E-Way's voice and speech.

"These bitch niggas got me. Don't give these niggas nothing. It's Kev—"

The phone went dead. Before E-Way could finish his statement Big Whitney hung up on Skyy.

***

"Hello? Hello?" Sky called over and over again. She tried calling back, but the voicemail picked up.

"Baby, what's wrong?" Trina asked from her seat across from Skyy at the kitchen table.

Skyy began to cry. "They got E-Way."

***

Big Whitney reached down and snatched E-Way to his feet. "Bitch, you gon' die tonight."

Big Whitney instructed Chuckie Boms to open the trunk to E-Way's Bentley. Together Big Whitney and Chuck picked E-Way up and put him in the trunk of his car.

"What we gon' do with his ass?" Kev asked as they all stood at the rear of the car looking down at E-Way.

"Y'all niggas is the worse bitch made niggas I've ever met," E-Way called out, beginning to cry. He had accepted the fact that he was about to die, but that wasn't why he was crying. He was fuming because these very niggas were the ones he would have given his life for and now this.

Big Whitney, who was obviously in charge of the conspiracy, didn't answer Kev's question. He closed the trunk and told Kev and Chuck to follow him. Big Whitney jumped into E-Way's Bentley and pulled away from the curb. He led Kev and Chuck to the old studio and bar site. He pulled into the back of the bar which was badly burned to a crisp. Kev and Chuck pulled in next to Big Whitney and parked. They all exited the cars and then walked around to the trunk where E-Way was.

E-Way had already made his peace with God and was wishing that whatever these bitch niggas were about to do, that they'd hurry up and do it. He could hear them talking near the trunk and knew that they had come to a stop but didn't know exactly where.

"Kev, grab that box out of the backseat," Big Whitney ordered.

Kev returned to the rear of the car carrying the brown box that Chuck had come out of the house with earlier. Big Whit popped the trunk. E-Way hadn't budged. He squinted from the beaming lights that filled the parking lot from light poles.

"You ready to die, Nigga?" Kev asked, looking down into E-Way's eyes.

"Nigga, fuck you, nothin' ass niggas!" E-Way yelled. Those were his last words.

Kev shot him a total of seven times in the face and head using a .40 caliber gun and emptying the remaining four rounds into E-Way's torso. Big Whitney, satisfied that E-Way was dead, opened the brown box and poured its contents inside of the trunk. The box contained white mice which Chuck used to feed his pet snake. The mice would literally eat E-Way's dead body or at least enough of it where he would unidentifiable.

Kev closed the trunk shut and then helped Big Whitney clean the door handles and interior of any finger prints. They jumped in the car with Chuck, leaving E-Way in the parking lot of the bar. Big Whitney took E-

Way's cell phone and threw it out of the window onto 7 Mile as they rode back to Chuck's house. They all filed into Chuck's basement and smoked blunts as if nothing had happened. Even if E-Way had given them the million dollars they'd requested, the still would have killed him out of envy.

~ Chapter 22 ~

Alina couldn't take any more pain and suffering. She was out of a job thanks to E-Way who boldly gave her cell phone to his girlfriend Skyy and threw her ass right under the bus! His recklessness had led to an ass whipping and her laying on the sofa watching episode after episode of Jerry Springer. Boredom had struck Alina, and she was sick and tired of being sick and tired. Flashbacks of E-Way controlled her train of thought. She remembered him fucking the shit out of her every other day, which apparently were only the days he wanted some information about Skyy. She was angry with him, but her pussy was pouncing against her panties at the thought of getting her rocks off with Skyy's man. There was nothing she hated more than a bitch that thought too highly of herself, and their lil' wrestling match made matters worse.

It's time to get off my ass and finish what I started, she thought. *The only way I could get back at Skyy is by catching everything that bitch goes after and making her life a living hell!* She squinted as she contemplated her plot. *I can…as a matter fact that's what I'll do – I'll call it Catching Hair! For starters, I'll steal all of her customers.*

Alina started surfing the web looking for tips and details on how to start her business. According to her memory, there was a building couple blocks up from Henry's that was unoccupied. Alina knew she needed help from that point, so she Googled an old friend. With the click of a button, all of her information came up along with her current cell phone number. She dialed the number, and after waiting a few rings Cimone picked up on the other end.

"Hello, Cimone speaking"

"Hey Cimone, this Alina."

"Who?"

"Alina, Girl! Bitch, don't act like you don't remember me! I used to fuck with yo' black ass cousin Danny."

"Oh Alina, the cute mixed bitch, I remember you."

"I haven't heard from you in so long. How you find me?"

"I know, right? We haven't seen each other in about three years. I actually found you on Google. I typed your name and all your information came up, along with your phone number," she explained. "Are you still into the real estate business?"

"Yes, I am. It's been about to be four years now. Why you ask?"

"Well for starters, I'm trying to open up the beauty salon and it's this building down the street from Henry's that I wanted to take a look at," she told her.

"I think I know the building you're talking about. I used to go to Henry's. What can I do to help?" Cimone answered, offering her assistance.

"Since you're a real estate agent I need your help to take me through the proper procedure of getting in that building."

"I believe I can do that, but I will need all your information to start the process. Matter fact, what you doin' now?"

"Shit, Girl, sitting here watching TV."

"Well, why don't you meet me down at the Waffle House so you can get started and we can talk about old times," Cimone suggested.

"Yeah, I can do that. I'll meet you there in about 35 minutes," she said and hung up the phone.

Alina wanted to look cute, knowing that Cimone was a cute bitch herself. She went upstairs to get herself together and started off by showering. A couple minutes, later she was headed to her closet and putting on a Michael Kors lace dress, Jimmy Choo shoes, and to top it off she wore a Michael Kors watch with the matching purse. She looked in the mirror once more to remind herself of how beautiful she looked. On that note, Alina got into her 2007 black Nissan Altima and drove towards her destination listening to Mary J. Blige featuring Drake *Mr. Wrong.*

Along the way, she passed her old job and saw her booth was taken. Everybody was laughing and having a good time. She saw Nicky talking to Skyy which could only mean he wanted details, or it was club night at Henry's - that alone put a big smile on her face. What turned that frown upside down was that bitch Skyy, who she hated the most. Before reaching her destination she rode past Henry's noticing that the building she had her eye on still had the for sale sign out front.

She pulled in the Waffle House parking lot trying to find somewhere to park. Due to rush hour business the place was crowded. After searching, she finally found a place to park and to her amazement it was right on the side of Cimone. She didn't even see Alina pulled in, she was sitting back in her car scrolling through her iPhone 6 until she jumped at the sound of tapping on her window.

"Bitch, you scared the shit out of me!" Cimone yelled with excitement as stepped out of the car with confidence, because just like Alina she thought she was pretty as she could be.

Cimone stood 5 foot 4 inches, butterscotch complexion, and she had cute dimples with a walk that says "I'm in control." Her hair came to her back, she had a petite body frame with a nice set of C cups, and her ass spoke up for her whole body. Her cute face put you in the mind of Black Chyna. Cimone had good taste; she wore a cotton blue Michael Costello dress with some black Giuseppe heels. Her eyes gazed through Chanel frames and her wrist boasted a matching watch. She wasn't the type of girl to sit on her ass and wait on handouts; she was willing to go out and make some moves of her own to get paid. She had three lovely kids – two boys and a girl. Her kids alone made her want to get up every day and get to the money. Cimone had the mind of a boss bitch and a hustle of a dope boy.

"Hey, Bitch! You look so good!" Alina yelled with a smile.

"Nah, Bitch, you the one that looks good with your mix bred ass!" Cimone said as she embraced Alina. "C'mon girl let's go in here before we don't have anywhere to say."

They made their entrance and were greeted by a waitress. All heads follow their every movement from the time they arrived to the time they sat down. Men were breaking their necks trying to look at Alina and Cimone.

"First let's handle our business. I need to know what it is you're trying to do and how you trying to go about doing it," Cimone said as she glanced briefly at the menu, then set it aside.

"Okay…as you already know I'm trying to open up a beauty salon. I want to get the building that's for sale up the street from Henry's. I have 26,000 dollars saved up from doing hair." Alina explained.

"In order to process all your information and see if you meet the requirements, we'll have to get your credit checked and go from there," Cimone said while reaching into her bag. "I have a home girl who's pretty decent with shit like that. Write your name, date of birth, and Social Security number down and I'll have her check the building out for you," she directed as she handed Alina a pen and small notepad.

Alina wrote all her information on the notepad and gave it to Cimone just as the waitress walked up to take their orders. They both ordered an all-star meal with orange juice. Then Cimone wasted no time in calling her friend to run a credit check on Alina.

"Bitch what do you want now?" Fruity answered.

Fruity was Cimone's gay homeboy and they have been knowing each other like forever. He was smart as hell and had three college degrees with one being a Master's degree. He spent his time doing hair and doing shit on the side for Cimone to make some extra money. He was gay as gay could be. He dressed like a woman, talked like a woman, and even looked like a woman. Everything he wore was skintight no matter if it was his socks, shirts, pants, or underwear. One thing about Fruity…he kept it a whole lot realer than some of the undercover street punks that were running around the area, and he could put a smile on the devil's face.

"I need you, Girl," Cimone told Fruity.

"Bitch, tell me some shit I don't know," he replied.

"Bitch, quit it you doin' too much now."

Fruity started laughing uncontrollably. "I miss you girl! Where you at? I'm bored and you know I was just playing with you."

"Girl, I'm up here at the Waffle House with a friend who I'm trying to help, but she need a few things done to see where she stands," Cimone answered.

"Got damn, Bitch! Every time you leave from around me you get sensitive as hell. Let me find out you trying to start a help-a-hoe foundation."

"Boy, I meant Girl... Can you do me a favor?"

"Bitch, call me another boy and watch me come to Waffle House and beat them waffles clean up out your little pretty ass!" Fruity snapped.

Cimone couldn't help but laugh. "I'm bout to text you the person's information and I'm a send you the building information too. I'm a need you to get right on this," she instructed.

"Got damn bitch, you act like this bitch is a celebrity. You need to be rushing her ass because you don't rush me. I got a man, and Bitch, you don't look nothing like him," Fruity ranted. "Send me the info before I change my mind."

"You should already have it. Check your messages and hit me right back." They ended their phone call and Cimone and Alina started talking girl talk.

"So what makes you want to open up a beauty salon?" Cimone inquired.

"For the past seven years or so I've been doing hair. I fell in love with it and been doing it right up until the last job I had," Alina answered.

"If you don't mind me asking, what happened at your last job? Did you quit or something?"

"Long story short… me and this bitch named Skyy didn't see eye to eye. We had our differences, but me and the bitch man end up fucking, which led to me giving him information on the bitch. See, the girls in the shop have this day (every Thursday) where they all go to Henry's. Her man E-way had suspicions of her cheating, so he had me do a follow up on her. I only did it because I hate the bitch and it was a reward for it." Alina explained. "Anyway, I catch the bitch in the act of tongue kissing, and letting this stripper named Chris put his hand damn near in her asshole on camera. I bring it to this nigga E-Way's attention - he take my whole fucking phone and give it to the bitch. All hell broke loose when I got back to work! That's the reason I'm naming my shop Catching Hair...because I'm trying to catch everything that bitch got from her man to her clientele and whatever the fuck that bitch get her hands on!"

"Girl, you wild as a mothafucka! I fucks with you…just remind me never to bring my man around you." They both busted out in laughter.

"Nah, it ain't nothin' like that. She just thought she was too much," Alina rationalized. "Don't get me wrong, the bitch bad. They say we look alike, but I think otherwise. Anyway, she misused her blessings, so that bitch deserve to be taught a lesson."

"It's some arrogant bitches out here…gotta watch for them types." Cimone's phone rung. "Talk to me."

"Bitch that girl credit badder than Kevin Hart's checking account."

"Bitch stop it," Cimone said laughing hard as hell. "Okay, what can you do for her about the building?"

"Well let's see here…them folks want 179,000 dollars for their building, 36,000 of it will get her stated, and other than that she better go holla at them bitches from *Set It Off* and try to make something shake."

"Bitch you need to cut it out (crazy ass). I know you the tax queen, so take all the shit off you added and let me know what's what," Cimone told Fruity, trying to cut through the bullshit.

"Owwee, Bitch! I tell you the truth, you fucking with my money now. But okay, she gon' need 30,000 dollars and a new friend if she fuck this up!" Fruity warned. "Not to be nosey, but what do she need it for?"

"She trying to start her own beauty salon."

"Tell her I said I need a booth if she make this happen," he said, seeing a possible opportunity in it for himself.

"Bitch, now you interfering with my business!"

"Bitch I got my own clientele. Yours wanna borrow a hairdo until they get paid? (With they first of the month asses)."

"Bitch bye. I'll call you back later. Do what I asked you," Cimone insisted.

"It's already done. All you have to do is meet with the owner," Fruity said as he texted her a few more details.

'Okay, bye," Cimone said with a sigh. "Bitch, this hoe is something else, but that's my dog. She said it will cost 30,000 dollars to get you started and 179,000 total."

"I told you I only have 26,000 dollars," Alina said in a disappointed tone.

"Don't worry about that…but since we're doing favors for favors I want to know if me and Fruity could come work in your shop part time."

"Girl, who is Fruity?"

"My home girl, who I just got off the phone with."

"So she is a he?"

"Yep, and I love that he/she to death," Cimone made clear.

"Why would I turn y'all down?" Alina asked. "I mean at least y'all trying to help a sister."

"Bitch, don't worry about the other money. Get your shop up and running and we'll see what's up when you get it together. We can go meet the owner of the building now."

They both left the restaurant after calling Mrs. Johnson. She was the one that owned the building. They followed each other to the location and sat at the building waiting for Mrs. Johnson to arrive.

"This bitch having us waiting forever! She told us 30 minutes and here it is a hour and 15 minutes later and she still haven't came," Cimone complained.

"It's hot as hell out here. She playing games," Alina added. "I could be at home watching Jerry Springer."

"No, no, no, Bitch… You're not going back down that lane. We came too far, it's time to get the paper," Cimone urged as she continued to watch for Mrs. Johnson. "Girl, that look like Fruity mustang," she said pointing toward the street.

"I'm sorry I'm late for the grand finale, but just be glad I showed up," Fruity announced. "Bitch did you miss me?" he said to Cimone. "And you must be Alina. I see something in you that I like already. You a snatch-a-bitch."

"Excuse me!" Alina said.

"Girl, you don't know none about girl talk…you a snatch-a-bitch man from her the minute she ain't looking."

She started laughing hard as hell. "Girl I like him already."

"Oh hell nah, Cimone! Hold my purse," he said in a fake fighting pose. "You didn't tell her I'm just as much a woman as she is?"

"Fruity you need to stop your shit," Cimone told him. "Do you got to be goofy everywhere you go?"

"As long as you around its always gon' be a goofy moment with your short ass."

"Don't start that shit out here," Cimone replied as she rolled her eyes playfully.

He smiled and sang along to the Panda song by Designer, while twerking in his size 12 jeans. They all couldn't help but to laugh at his nonsense.

Meanwhile, another car approached and this time it was Mrs. Johnson. She was tall and black with a cute face like Sanaa Lathan! She had bodacious curves fitting her Donna Karen skirt with the blouse to match.

She didn't seem like your average woman. She was like a classy ghetto broad with a couple chips stacked up, rolling in a 2017 Impala.

Fruity was the first one to greet her. "Hi, Mrs. Johnson. You're taller than I expected you to be."

"Fruity, where's your manners?" Cimone interjected. "I'm sorry, Mrs. Johnson. You have to excuse people like this."

"It's alright," Mrs. Johnson replied. "Out of the three of you, who's Alina?"

"I am," Alina said clearing her throat, still trying to deflect Fruity's negative comment.

"We can take a quick tour if you like," Mrs. Johnson offered as she unlocked the door to the old building. She guided them inside and they all took a tour through the place.

"It's bigger in here than I thought," said Alina, scanning the room.

"It smells like oral sex in here. I'm pretty sure it haven't got to you yet," Fruity said referring to Mrs. Johnson and her height.

"It can use some remodeling, but that's minor right now. You have to get you some supplies and some appliances," Cimone said, nudging Fruity aside. "We'll take it!" she announced as she wrote out a check for 30,000 dollars and handed it to Mrs. Johnson.

"Here's your key," Mrs. Johnson said, handing a set of keys to Alina. "Your official paperwork will be mailed to you within 5 to 10 business days. Thank you and good luck on your salon."

"You're welcome. You have a nice day," Alina replied.

"Come back and see us, with all them beady beads on the back of your neck," Fruity said.

"I will Jawana man," Mrs. Johnson said, waving as she left.

"Oh no that I heffa didn't, with her Madea looking ass!"

"I see now Fruity gon' be a handful," Alina said while still chuckling at the joke he made.

"Well, Bitch…we got some cleaning up to do, but first let me tell you about the money situation. You go ahead and use your money to get this place fixed up, and hit me on the back end when shit starts picking up for you. Remember you only got 6 chairs - 2 already occupied, so Bitch, do your thing and get some reliable workers."

~ Chapter 23 ~

Alina had been ripping and running trying to get the shop in order. She moved furniture around and redecorated tiles. She had the place looking like brand-new. Fruity and Cimone hung up banners, balloons, and flowers; they put everything out front for Alina's grand opening. She had filled all the chairs that weren't occupied, and put an extra chair in the shop for a barber. She had hired four new workers: Shuntae, Kira, Juicy, and Horace.

Shuntae was a cute big black woman (BBW); she always kept herself up and stayed on the ground. Most people got along with her, but a few didn't because they couldn't put up with her mouth. It's like she had no filter about the things she said. Kira was the fly type that always dressed pretty and made sure she was up on the latest fashion. Kira had a drug habit. She stayed high and loved to be seen. Juicy was your hype girl. She knew how to keep the party alive and keep tensions from building up between others. Her name came from the ass she carried on her back. She had a daughter she loved, who meant the world to her. She was all about staying fly, but she was more than willing to partake in a good fight. Horace on the other hand was a laid back dude who loved to smoke and make money. He had two brothers and one sister who he had to be a role model to. He stayed out of trouble and cut hair on the side, but don't let the clippers fool you because he was born bout that life.

On the day of the grand opening, cars passed by honking horns while others stopped by to congratulate Alina on her new business. She even got visits from some of Skyy's clientele, whom she bribed to start coming there for half off prices. The shop instantly flooded with people and conversations.

"Thank you, girl. I'm a bring all my business to you. My hair looks marvelous," Trina said.

"Please do, Honey, because you look fabulous," Shuntae said.

As soon as Trina left, the gossip came right behind her.

"Girl, that bitch should've tried to get the next role in *Friday* playing Felicia," Fruity said.

"She was ugly. She ain't have not one side burn," Juicy consigned.

"Girl, you bitches a mess," Alina said, shaking her head.

"Then she had on them long ass shoes...Jarrett from Subway could've told you that bitch wore a footlong," Kira added.

The whole shop was laughing, even the kids who were lined up to get their hair cut.

"Are we about finished?" Dena asked Cimone.

"Oh, Girl you cute! I got you in the game. You gonna have to come back and see me," Cimone replied as she swiveled her chair around so she could see the mirror.

"I sure will, Boo," she answered as she examined her hair with satisfaction.

Fruity was doing twist locs in April's hair, and she kept fidgeting.

"Excuse me. If you don't stop jumping like you got the jungle fever, I ain't gone be able to part your hair right."

"My bad, Bitch. I'm tender headed, plus this nigga keep irritating me asking me the same fucking questions," April said adjusting herself one last time.

"Well I'm a need you to tell him to call you back later when you look like a new person."

"What you trying to say, Fruity?"

"Girl, get out yo' feelings and turn your head to the left."

"I think he trying to say you look like a chicken head," Shuntae said instigating.

"Bitch, you trying to start some shit," Fruity said.

Horace's phone started ringing. "Hello."

It was his brother Ron Jay. "I like LeBron and his squad tonight," Ron Jay said. It was game 7 of Cleveland and Golden State, and Cleveland had fought all the way back from a 1-3 deficit.

"Aight, I'll take Steph Curry, we can bet 1000 dollars none too heavy," Horace replied.

"We can do that. Everybody going to mama house, hit through when you get a chance."

"Bet it up. I'll fall through when I get off," Horace said and ended the call.

"I know you just didn't bet on Steph Curry, because LeBron about to whoop that ass tonight," Juicy said.

"LeBron ain't on shit. He known for fucking up."

"I'm riding with LBJ tonight too," Shuntae said, cosigning Juicy.

Kira, Alina, Cimone, and Fruity were all going for Steph Curry.

The crowd was narrowing down in the shop and the day was coming to an end.

"Bitch, we need to go turn up," Shuntae said.

"I don't know, Girl. I had a long day," Kira replied.

"That bitch ready to go suck her nigga dick and get high," Shuntae said, pointing her finger in Kira's direction.

"Fuck you, Shuntae!"

"Well, I want to congratulate everyone on their first day's success." Alina interrupted. "Business did really good and I hope we can keep it up."

"Here she go with this Wendy Williams shit," Fruity said.

Everybody started laughing.

"While everybody laughing, I'm a need y'all to know that booth day (which is rent) will be on Sundays," Alina informed.

"Nie this hoe want tithes and offerings," Fruity said.

"Do you want us to wear a sundress or some slacks and pass the collection plate around too?" Shuntae asked.

Everybody was laughing so hard until some of them had tears in their eyes. Horace was so high he was laughing but there wasn't any sound coming out. Alina sat there looking annoyed, but with a couple of chuckles because she enjoyed the environment. It was like she was around her favorite group of people and didn't want it to end. Cimone enjoyed the moment also. She sat there soaking up everybody's personality and thought to herself that Catching Hair was about to be put on the map - big time! Juicy was ready for the turn up. She made more than enough money to do whatever she desired.

"Bitch, what everybody gone do? My lil girl got a babysitter and I really want to go out," Juicy said.

"We know you ready to go throw that ass in a circle," Fruity said.

"Loose booty Juicy," Shuntae said, laughing. Those words alone made Juicy start twerking it like she had her own radio in her head.

"I know she ain't trying to outdo me. I'm the twerk queen in this mothafucka," Fruity said as he threw his hands in the air and started vibrating both of his legs while looking at the invisible ass he thought he had.

Horace spit his drink out. "Hell nah! I gotta go."

The shop was full of laughter and the turn up felt real. The excitement Fruity had given everyone made them want to go out; however, Horace opted out after what he had just witnessed.

"We all know what Horace is trying to do, but with Kira...it ain't no secret that, that hoe trying to go shoot up, smoke, or snort," Shuntae said, trying to be funny.

"Good night y'all, cause this bitch don't know what to say out her mouth," Kira snapped as she gathered her things.

"What I'm trying to do?" Horace asked with a grin.

"Get high and go pay your brother that stack, because LeBron and Kyrie just put that work in on that ass."

"Yeah, I gotta go catch up with some of my fam. I know they ass drunk as hell, passing hella blunts around. I'll catch up with y'all tomorrow," Horace said on his way out the door.

They all said their goodbyes to Kira and Horace.

"Y'all bitches ready to go get it in?" Cimone asked.

"Hell yeah. We need to gone make our move so we can get us a good spot," Alina said.

"Is we riding five deep? If so, we can burn the gas out of Shuntae truck," Fruity said.

"Y'all better put up 3 dollars a head. If not, we'll be piling up in Fruity lil ass Mustang: 2 in the front, 1 on the hood, and 2 lapped up," Shuntae said as she was trying to catch her breath from laughing.

They all knew the club was about be packed due to Cleveland bringing the championship back home and crowning themselves the 2016 Champs. To avoid lapping up, then decided they would pay Shuntae the 3 dollars and ride out. Alina locked the doors and turned on the alarm system as they were leaving. Shuntae pulled up at a gas station and everybody started looking around as if they didn't know Shuntae was about to ask for that gas fare.

"Ain't no need for y'all hoes to get quiet now. Shit, you bitches better empty out them purses and scrape up 3 dollars worth of change or our asses will be right here panhandling," Shuntae announced.

"This bitch right here is something else. I know that gas meter ain't broke with her trifling ass! This heffa sitting on a full tank of gas and charging us 3 dollars for hoe fare. Ain't this bout a bitch?" Fruity said.

"Man, how in the hell did we get these two together? They ass is hilarious," Juicy said holding her stomach to keep from pissing on herself.

"Got damn, Bitch! You trying to pimp a bitch out them lil few dollars?" Alina asked.

"She probably trying to come up with some lunch money," Cimone said.

"Hold up, Cimone. That ain't even for us. I tried to spare you and you still gone jump in the line of fire?" Shuntae said.

"My bad, Bitch. I had to get that one off."

"Ain't no need to apologize now. If her ass go get a x-ray right now, they gone find 6 large fries, 6 extra-large combos, and the doctor she ate for trying to x-ray her," Fruity joked.

They all laughed their asses off, even Shuntae. She finally got out to go pay for the gas. Fruity followed her in and came back out with some gum and some wine coolers. They all started sipping their drinks and passing around 3 high powered kush blunts that Juicy and Cimone had rolled to perfection. The parking lot to Henry's was so packed you could barely park out there.

"This bitch live tonight," Cimone said.

"It's Thursday night, Girl," Alina said. *Oh shit,* she thought to herself. That meant Skyy and Nicky, Maria, Erica, and the rest of her friends were going to be there. She really wasn't tripping, because she knew her home girls weren't about to let shit happen to her. Alina really wanted to see Chris, so she could use the power of the pussy on him and lure him right into her plans to make Skyy miserable. Just in case anything got crazy she brought her pepper spray with her. Everybody was geeked off the weed they had just blazed and they were making their way to the door.

"How y'all doing today?" the bouncer asked.

"We doing fine," Fruity said flirtatiously.

He laughed and let them through the metal detectors. Alina was the only one who beeped off. She gave an innocent ass smile and he told her that she was cool. As they made their entrance, you could see big black dick slanging everywhere. They instantly started reaching for their singles and other bills.

"This is my type of party," Shuntae said. "It's big dick all around this mothafucka! They about to get all my lil hair money," she said as she laughed at her own comment.

"Bitch let's go get some drinks," Fruity said as he pulled Juicy by the arm guiding her through the heavy crowd. Fruity looked up and saw this guy who looked to be a homosexual staring daggers at him in a seductive way.

"Fruity, I see you got a fan club already," Juicy said while giving a fake smile to the girl that was with the guy. "I think you should go meet him," she snickered sarcastically.

"Bitch, am I friendly?" Fruity asked just as the guy began to approach him.

"Excuse me," the guy said, reaching in for a handshake. "This is my friend Marie and my name is Nicky. I couldn't help but notice you from afar. You are very attractive and I want to know if you and your friend would like to join us."

With a big grin on his face, Fruity replied, "I'm sorry but I don't do women. My friend might, but I'd be willing to take my chances with you any day."

Nicky was hot in the pants and was ready for some boy on boy action.

"Hi my name is Juicy," she said has she introduced herself to Nicky's friend.

"Hi Juicy, I'm Marie," she said as she leaned in closer so that she could be heard over the loud music. "My friend wasn't on any orgy type shit. He just wanted to get acquainted with your friend. Not saying that you're an ugly girl or anything, because I wooould like to see what it's like to fuck a girl."

"Don't pay her any mind, Juicy. That's just the liquor talking. She ain't never talked like that before, Honey," Nicky said, rolling his eyes.

"Oh, she alright," Juicy replied. "I ain't never fucked with a female before, but she tempting me."

Juicy and Marie ordered drinks and exchanged numbers while Fruity and Nicky excused themselves, and slid off into the crowd somewhere on the other side of the club. Shuntae, Alina, and Cimone were changing their big bills for singles, so they could dish them out to the strippers. Alina had spotted Chris looking in her direction. She instantly got the chills because it caught her off guard. The whole time she had been looking for him, but it seemed as if he was looking for her also; and to make the situation even more convenient...he approached her.

"This can't be happening," Chris said with an awkward frown on his face. "You got the nerve to show your face in here after what happened with you and Skyy. You know that woman is crazy about me."

"Listen Chris, I'm sorry. I didn't mean for that to blow out of proportion like that."

"But it did, Woman. You almost got me fired; and besides that, Skyy's crew is in here tonight. Lucky for you, she ain't in here with them!"

"That's good to know. Maybe we can go talk in private, so people won't walk up on our conversation and make shit seem bigger than what it already is?"

"Well, I guess..." Chris said as he scanned the room for options of privacy. "Follow me," he said as he turned to her friends. "I'll bring her back to you just I found her," he told Shuntae and Cimone.

"Alright, just make sure you bring some of them strippers built like you back," Shuntae said.

Chris walked off grinning with Alina in his shadow.

"A bathroom, Chris?" Alina said, rolling her eyes. "This the only private area you can find?"

"I mean, unless you want to go to a private room with a lot of folks fucking and sucking – we can..." Chris answered.

She didn't even think twice. They both went into a bathroom stall and instantly Alina grabbed Chris's manhood and stuffed it in her hot, warm mouth.

"Damn I didn't know this what you wanted to talk about," Chris said as his eyes roll back in his head.

Sounds of Alina slurping was all that could be heard in the stall. She came up for a brief second and said, "Damn, Boy. You got a big monster, don't you?"

Alina took all of Chris in her mouth - she was gagging and all. Chris felt so good he wanted to recruit her on his team. She sucked the tip of his dick, twirling her tongue around in a circular motion. Then she lifted his dick and put both of his balls in her mouth while she gently sucked them simultaneously. Chris tried to maintain his cool, but felt like he was drifting off into heaven for a few minutes. Alina sucked his dick so good, he had busted a mega load in her mouth that ran down her cheeks onto her chin. He took his finger and wiped the excess nut from her chin and stuck it in her mouth. As she licked his finger clean, he begged for some pussy. He imagined that if the head was this good, the pussy had to be pure ecstasy. He turned her around, lifted her skirt, and pulled her boy shorts to the side revealing her soaking wet pussy. She was so wet he slid right in stretching her walls a tad bit.

"Oooh, Chris, that big mothafucka feel good."

"You feel good too, Baby Girl. You like this dick?"

Ahhh, ahhh, ahhh was all that could be heard coming from her. He was giving her long, deep strokes to make her feel all the dick he had to offer.

"Chris, we need you to report to the stage," the DJ announced over the loud speaker.

"Fuck! This pussy is good, but I got to go."

"No. Don't pull it out. It feels so good."

"But, Baby I got a job to do. Here, take my card and we'll get together very soon and finish up what we started. I promise."

"Tonight!" Alina said as she adjusted her outfit, trying to get situated.

"You know Skyy's entourage is in the building. She just might walk up in here at any time. Let's take a raincheck and I'll make it up to you," Chris replied as he walked toward the door.

"Oh yeah, I forgot about your lil fan club," Alina said sarcastically. "She still fucking with you even after the fact? You know what...never mind."

"Alina?" Nicky taunted as he came out a bathroom stall wiping his mouth with Fruity right behind him.

She covered her mouth in disbelief. "Oh my God" were the only words she could find to say.

"I done seen enough. I'm gone," Chris said as he left the bathroom.

"Bitch, you just gone keep back-dooring that girl, trying to get everything she got huh?" Nicky said with a look of disgust on his face.

"You damn right! That bitch and think she too much, so I got a trick for her ass."

"Bitch, what is he talking bout?" Fruity asked.

"Long story...we'll talk at work tomorrow at the shop."

"What shop?" Nicky inquired.

"Her shop - she got her own shop," Fruity responded.

"Hold up, rewind this shit - skrrrrrkkk. You mean to tell me you successful bitch and I don't know about it?"

"I thought you was taking your best friend side and you don't want shit to do with me."

"I was taking her side cause you was wrong, but you could've at least sent a bitch a text or something, heffa! I'm proud of you, Bitch."

"Thank you, Nick Nick!"

Chapter 24

Skyy had been really standoffish ever since E-Way's disappearance. There was still no word and she wasn't feeling much like socializing. Nicky had invited her and Trina to Henry's last night to take her mind off of things, but she wasn't feeling up to it, so Trina stayed behind to keep her company. She was supposed to be meeting up with Chris after he got off work, but she stood him up. She was thinking maybe Chris could take her mind off the situation with E-Way, but the thought of Chris just made her feel guilty more than anything.

When she got to the shop the next morning she wasn't herself. She was trying to perk herself up and be optimistic, but it was difficult under the circumstances. Nicky immediately recognized the fact that Skyy was down and tried to change the mood with some good old fashion messy ass gossip.

"Bitch, how bout I met me a new tenderoni in the club last night..." Nicky bragged.

"Who's the lucky somebody?" Skyy asked trying to fall back into the norm.

"His name is Fruity, Girl."

Skyy strained out a giggle. "What kind of name is Fruity?"

"Bitch, don't do him. His name tells it all."

"I see you kind of defensive about somebody you just met. Let me find out he tapped that ass in one night," Skyy said trying to find some enthusiasm for the topic.

"You talking bout the same way you defensive about Chris?" Nicky reminded Skyy. "And yes... He rocked my world and I sucked him dry. Oh and speaking of Chris - details, Bitch!"

"Nothing happened with us last night. I stood him up. I ended up falling asleep on the couch. I'll give him a call later though."

"You probably need to call him, Girl. I could've swore I caught a glimpse of something between him and that bitch Alina last night," Nicky said being messy.

"Let me find out that bitch trying to be in my way again! I'm a whoop that ass from old to new," Skyy said with resentment because she blamed Alina on some level for everything that was going on with E-Way.

"Bitch, the girl holding a grudge. She said she got a trick for yo' ass."

"Oh yeah, I need to find that hoe and beat her ass into a coma!"

"Damn bitch, you want her dead, don't it?" Nicky said with a giggle.

"Nah, she can live. I just want her not to be able to interfere with nobody else relationship."

Marie and Erica walked into the shop smiling from ear to ear.

"What y'all bitches so happy about?" Nicky asked, looking them both up and down.

"Damn can we get in the door, Prince?" Erica replied as she observed the spoiled look on his face. She laughed and sat her bag down.

"Bitch you errrks my nerves, but hey Marie. I see you by yourself," Nicky said, glancing over his shoulder at Erica.

"Hey, Boo," she replied.

Erica caught on, so she made a circle with her fingers and took one finger on the other hand and went in and out of the circle. After that, she pointed at Nicky to let him know he needs to go somewhere and get fucked in the ass hole, and leave her alone. He rolled his eyes and started back talking to Skyy.

"Yeah anyway... I hear Alina got her own shop now."

"She got her own shop?" Skyy repeated. "That was quick! Wonder how many dicks that hoe had to suck to put that in motion…"

"Yes, bitch. Fruity told me, but I got to get more details."

"Please do, cause I want to pay her a little visit."

"Bitch, you can't do that. That is not professional."

Skyy scanned Nicky with the side-eye, rolled her eyes. "Stealing pictures of bitches and fucking around with they nigga on the low is not professional."

"You right! Somebody need to teach that lil sneaky ass bitch a lesson," Nicky consigned. "Can't you tell that the girl envy you?"

"Envy my ass! She gone envy herself into another ass whooping."

"You know what? Fuck that conversation. Marie, how did things go with you and Juicy last night?" Nicky asked.

"I know you're dying to get the details," Marie said in a teasing tone. "Bitch, we had a few drinks and drunk each other afterwards."

"That's all it took…for a cute project bitch to bring that wild side out of you."

"Hold up! Juicy is a girl?" Skyy asked.

"Yeah, she my newest work yet," Marie answered. "Bitch, I was drunk as hell and Juicy had me soaking wet for some reason. I don't know why, but that girl got this pussy jumping."

"Ewwwwww! Nobody don't want to hear all that, Bitch. Your details you can keep." Skyy replied.

Marie laughed out loud and proceeded to brag to everyone about how her first experience with a woman was amazing. She made it clear that she was definitely fucking with Juicy from that point on. Meanwhile, Joe was kind of standoffish. He started feeling uncomfortable with everybody, because of the hint Nicky tossed around about him. He would cut hair every now and then, but mostly he would call in or slow drag to work. The shop was slowing down on business and very few were coming in, so the soup about the club last night was basically the highlight of the day. Nicky was doing a customer's hair, but had excused himself to go gossip for the umpteenth time.

"Please sir or madam, could you please finish my hair? I have somewhere to be very soon," Ms. Janet announced.

Nicky snapped his fingers while rolling his eyes. "Don't you see me talking, Grandma?"

"Grandma? I got your grandma you sissy bitch!"

"Bitch! Oh, hell nah... Hold up! I'm bout to whoop this Florida Evans looking ass bitch."

"Un-Un, Un-Un! This is a place of business and not a wrestling ring, so y'all need to just chill," Skyy demanded.

Erica started chanting, "Jer-ry, Jer-ry, Jer-ry" trying to egg on a fight.

"I don't have to take this shit. I'm going to Catching Hair, where they treat their customers with some respect," Ms. Janet yelled.

"Fuck no. Get yo' old ass on and take that moth ball ass stench with you," Skyy snapped.

"That bitch smell like she run a vet full of cats," Erica added.

"All of you need to be taught some respect! Besides, it looks like y'all running a function junction in this mothafucka, starring Ray Gay," Ms. Janet said as she walked out of the shop.

"Ray Gay?" Erica joked. "She called you the reject Ray J. I had to laugh. She got you!"

"Bitch, one of these days..." Nicky said before he was cut off mid-sentence.

"What you gon' be a man?" Erica blurted out in a laughing fit, fueling Nicky up even more.

***

"Damn, last night was crazy as hell. Even Fruity got his virginity broke," Shuntae said mocking Fruity.

Alina busted out laughing, because she had a run-in with him and his lil snack cake Nicky. "Shhhhhh," Fruity said signaling to Alina not to spill the beans about what happened between him and Nicky.

"Hell nah, we ain't keeping no secrets up in here - not up in here got dammit," Shuntae said in a manly tone.

Just then, Cimone and Horace walked into the shop together laughing and giggling.

"Speaking of secrets...what y'all two got going on? Is there something that you mothafuckas want to tell everybody, while y'all he-he-n and ha-ha-n?" Fruity said trying to change the subject.

"Good morning my lovely friends. I see y'all up in here early this morning," Cimone said ignoring Fruity's inquiry.

It was 8 o'clock in the morning, and Horace's eyes were lit like a firecracker. He was high as hell.

"Damn, Horace! You ain't save a bitch nothing to smoke?" Shuntae asked.

"Hey, how everybody doing," Horace said as he glanced around the room in a manner which to acknowledge everyone present. "And yeah...I got us some ducked off for later," he added with a smile.

"That's what's up. Save a bitch from this sober world."

Kira walked in looking like she had a hangover from her drug of choice that she indulged last night. "Look what the needle shot out," Shuntae muttered under her breath but loud enough for others to hear.

"Shuntae I ain't trying to put up with your shit today," Kira said with a smile to let it be known that her statement was friendly.

They were one short from a full staff, and the outside parking lot was starting to get packed. Cars seemed to be coming out of nowhere. Children were lined up for haircuts, while mothers stood by waiting on them. They were taking walk-ins and booked appointments. The shop was buzzing!

"Can you cut me a phat back?" a kid asked.

"I can do whatever you want," Horace answered.

"Alright. Hook me up with a phat back, two parts on the right side of my head, and a clean line up."

"Boy, what the hell is a phat back?" the kid's mom asked.

"Some of the cool kids where em, Ma. I gotta hip you."

"Boy sit your young ass down. You still got milk behind your ears and shit marks in your draws. You talking bout hipping me..."

The entire shop broke out laughing.

"Dang Ma, you gon' put me on blast like that? I know you see that cute honey over there," the kid said jokingly referring to Alina.

Alina just laughed at the cute little remark that he made.

"Boy, you too much. That lady don't want no young boy who is still in the sixth grade with no money," his mom replied.

"No money?" The boy stood up and pulled out two thousand dollars in all hundreds.

The whole shop got quiet and started clearing their throats, letting the boy's mom know that he had proved her wrong.

"Boy, where in the hell you get all that money from?"

"Being in the sixth grade can teach you a lot about how to get money, Ma," the kid answered with a devious smirk on his face. His mom twisted his ear and pulled him out of the shop.

"Damn, kids grow up faster than a mothafucka these days," Horace said.

"He probably fucking all the lil sixth graders at his school," Fruity said.

"Not anymore," Kira said shaking her head. "His mama bout to peel his lil ass for a couple hundred."

The boy and his mom passed by Juicy on her way in the shop.

"What in the hell that lil boy did in here for his mama to be pulling his ear like a rubber band?" she asked as she walked in.

"Hey friend," Fruity said while reaching out to hug Juicy.

"What's up, Baby," Juicy said as she embraced Fruity. "Hey everybody. Good morning."

Everybody spoke back.

"Bitch, the lil boy just embarrassed his mama in here acting mannish. He in the sixth grade and she basically called him broke. He stunted on her and pulled out about 2,500 dollars," Fruity said.

"Nah, get the fuck out of here!"

"Yeah, Bitch…these lil preteens ain't playing," Fruity replied.

"I can take somebody over here," Juicy announced as she twisted her chair toward the crowd.

A young lady raised her hand anxiously.

"Come on, Baby."

"Um, can you do micros?"

"Why sure," Juicy answered knowing that the hairdo was high priced. "I charge 130 dollars, but to keep you as a client I'm a charge you 90 bucks."

"Oh, that's fine with me," the young lady agreed.

The bell at the top of the door rang indicating that someone had either entered or exited the shop.

"Good morning, everybody," Ms. Janet said.

"How you doing, Ms. Janet?" Alina said with a smile.

"Hey boo, I haven't seen you in a minute now. So, this is where you've been hiding out at."

"Yeah, this my shop," Alina said proudly.

"I see you left them thirsty, ungrateful bastards alone at the other beauty salon and did something on your own," Ms. Janet replied begrudgingly.

"Yeah, we had words or whatever, but what got you so hyped up?"

"Oh nothing, girl... That sissy bitch down there think he can do whatever he want, leave when he wanna leave while he on a client...I don't have time for that shit. I had somewhere to be."

Alina laughed at the thought of Skyy's customers getting fed up with their bullshit and leaving them to come to Catching Hair.

"Well, Ms. Janet, I have a fine group of workers. Since your hair is halfway done, I'm going to give you a free hairdo under one condition..."

"And what's the condition?"

"I want you to recommend my shop to all your friends, family, associates – whoever," Alina campaigned.

"That's all, Girl? Hell, I can do that with my eyes closed. I can start a boycott on her shit if that's the case."

"Deal," Alina said as she reached out for a handshake.

"Yep, deal."

"Did you have a good time last night?" Juicy asked Fruity.

"Ummmm..." Alina cut in. "I'm quite sure he did."

"Oh, please, Bitch! Like you're Miss Perfect," Juicy said. "Go ahead. We can exchange stories."

"C'mon now, Fruity... Wait till these lovely customers get out of earshot," Cimone suggested.

"Juicy, don't you got some hot gossip for us?" Shuntae asked.

"You know I do. I ain't got shit to hide, Bitch," Juicy answered. "While yo' crazy ass think you bout to put me on front street..."

Shuntae just laughed at the thought of Juicy figuring her out. Meanwhile, Ms. Janet finally got her hair finished and she looked like a new lady.

"Thank you, sugar," she told Alina.

"You're welcome, Ms. Janet."

She poked in the mirror and was astounded by the great job that Alina had done.

"Owwweee, Girl! You got me looking like...what's that girl's name with the bid ol' butt? Oh, Honey, Nicki Minaj! These young boys better watch out, cause Ms. Janet bout to go pay for some anaconda!"

The whole shop fell out laughing at Ms. Janet.

"Ms. Janet, you a mess, Honey! Them young boys gone put that anaconda on you and have you running for your diabetic meds," Shuntae said.

"Oh, Child, hush! Ms. Janet still know how to tootsie roll, cupid shuffle, and pop-lock-n-drop-it," she said as she started doing the tootsie roll in the middle of the shop.

"Oooh, Ms. Janet...you know you wrong," Fruity said.

"Alrighty, y'all...I enjoyed y'all and Ms. Janet will be back," she said as she left.

Everyone said their goodbyes to Ms. Janet, while still talking about the show she had just put on.

"Girl, Ms. Janet a mess," Cimone told Alina.

"Ain't she, Girl? But she gon' bring us a lot of business, with her loud mouth butt."

"Ms. Janet bout to go hurt somebody with all that booty she got," Kira said. "Anyway, when y'all going back to Henry's? I'm tired of being left out."

"Awwwh, you wanna come boo?" Juicy replied.

"Yes," she answered in the most childish voice ever.

"Girl, ain't no dope fiends in there, and them big dicks gone crush your little ass," Shuntae interjected.

"Shuntae, you always got something to say, with you hungry-hungry-hippo looking ass," Kira said while laughing uncontrollably. Juicy laughed with her, along with the rest of the shop. Shuntae played it off and laughed along also, but in reality Kira had just embarrassed her in front of everybody.

"You ready to go blaze up?" Horace asked Shuntae.

"Give me a second. I'm on my last braid."

Kira's eyes lit up at the thought of smoking. "Kira, you want to smoke with us?" Horace asked.

"You know I do."

The shop started to clear out and business was slowing down. Fruity was finishing up with the last customer, and it was time for gossip.

"Who that girl you was with, Juicy?" Cimone asked.

"You ain't waste no time, Bitch," Juicy said. "Her name is Marie. She my new lil fuck buddy."

"Fuck buddy?" Cimone repeated with a confused look on her face.

"Marie?" Alina asked.

"Yeah, I tried something new last night and I liked it. Regardless if she's a woman or not, she can eat it up better than most of these niggas!"

"I ain't gon' look at you different. Bitch, I still fucks with you," Cimone said.

"Marie? Bitch you let her turn you out!" Alina said.

"Actually, we turned each other out," Juicy replied in a bragging tone.

"That's my dog," Fruity said mocking Smokey off of the movie *Friday*.

Horace, Kira, and Shuntae all walked back in after relieving themselves for a smoke break.

"Look like we came back in at the right time," Shuntae said.

"So Fruity, let's hear what happened with you and Nicky," Alina said.

"Damn, Bitch! You all in my movie, but since you insist...me and Nicky connected at first sight. I wasn't feeling him, but when he made his approach I was like, *Damn, he fine as hell*. That's when we excused ourselves from Juicy and Marie and took it straight to the boom-boom room.

Girl, when I tell you the man can fuck and suck... He tickled the cat last night - had me moaning for dear life..."

"What's the boom-boom room, Fruity?" Alina asked.

"Bitch, the fuck box - the stall in the bathroom... I'm sure you had an experience back there too. But anyway, Nicky was wet as hell, and I fucked the hell out of him. When it was my turn, I showed out. I went mayhem on that ass. He was hollering like a lil bitch!"

Everybody was laughing expect for Horace, who couldn't ponder thought of two men going at it. He grabbed his keys and shook his head while heading for the door.

"Bye y'all," Horace said as he walked out.

They all said their goodbyes, and continued the conversation.

"Now your turn Alina," Fruity said sounding demanding.

"Well my lil experience was crazy. At first, we was just talking, but the noise level was increasing to the point you couldn't hear shit, so me and Chris went to the boom-boom room to get some privacy. Really I just wanted to get out the hating bitch's way who tried to knock my shine. He went to bringing up old shit, so I took it upon myself and grabbed that 12-inch monster out them boy shorts he wore and gave him the best head ever! He went to mumbling some shit, but he sounded retarded as hell - probably because I had his balls in my mouth and was sucking the life out of him," she said with a smirk. "He started begging me to stop, so he could feel how wet the pussy was. I didn't stop right away because I wanted to feel like I was in control. Then I turned around, bent over, and pulled my panties to the side. When I tell you the man's penis is thick as hell...he stretched my insides, but he slipped in me so smooth cause my pussy was wetter than Hurricane Katrina!" Alina laughed out loud. "He got a few strokes in and they announced him to come to the stage. That's when we came out and I saw Nicky wiping his mouth with Fruity right behind him."

"Bitch, I heard them ask for Chris because he was the main event," Cimone remembered.

"That was at the time I was getting my back blown out."

"Bitch, you a certified freak, ain't you?" Fruity said.

"I gotta get me some dick," Kira said.

"Me too, Girl," Fruity consigned.

"Me too. We'll see y'all bitches tomorrow," Shuntae said as the tree of them walked out together.

Cimone stayed with Alina to help her clean up and lock up.

"Bitch, that story got me horny as hell. I'm bout to go put that work in on my baby daddy, with his good dick having ass," Cimone said.

"You and your baby daddy got a good sex relationship?"

"I mean yeah...at first he'll bust a nut in about 15 minutes. Now I done learned that dick though. I suck him until he gets that first nut off, then he come back with the pound game. Anyway, why you ask? I told you I ain't bringing him around you. You like to suck the life out people," Cimone said sarcastically, referring to the story Alina had just told.

"Bitch, stop doing that. I told you I ain't gone fuck over nobody I fucks with. You alright with me, and I'm starting to like you a lot more."

"Hell nah! Here you go with this Marie and Juicy shit!"

They both laughed as they headed out the door and locked up the shop.

Chapter 25

After all the stories, Cimone headed home. She had a plan to cook for her man Jaquel, and put the kids in the tub and off to bed. Then on to an evening of freaky loving…

Jaquel was one of those project hustlers who was ready to make a dollar whether it made sense or not, but he also played a big role in his kids' lives. They had three kids together: 1 girl (Ja'mone) and 2 boys (Darius and Ta'darius). Jaquel was one who always put family first, but family wasn't putting him first so he broke away from the negative shit and started a beautiful family with Cimone.

Just as she walked into the big 4-bedroom house they shared, she was greeted by her kids who ran to her grabbing on her and hugging her. Jaquel got up from playing Madden 16 on the PlayStation 4 and kissed Cimone.

"Hey, Baby."

"Hey, Daddy. What's up? Y'all hungry?"

"Yessss," the kids screamed.

"Y'all said that like Daddy haven't been feeding y'all."

"They ate about 4 hours ago. They might be hungry again."

"What does everybody want to eat?"

The kids all said, "Macaroni and chicken."

"Oh y'all think y'all smart, huh? Did Daddy tell y'all to say that?"

Nobody answered Cimone because they knew that snitching wasn't allowed in their house. Everybody just smiled.

"Oh okay, everybody gone hold a code of silence on me," Cimone said, smiling. She playfully slapped Jaquel upside the head as she walked toward the kitchen. The children laughed at their actions.

"Thank you, Baby," Jaquel said with a smile. "The chicken should already be thawed. It's in the sink."

"Alright, Daddy."

As she was setting up to season the chicken and taking down the dishes she would be serving on, Jaquel came up behind her and hugged her waist while putting his dick on her ass.

"Baby, I missed you."

"I missed you too, Daddy."

"How bad you miss Daddy?" he asked.

"Oh, I'm about to show you how bad I missed you soon as we get the children fed and put to bed."

"Oh yeah?" he asked while planting kisses on her neck. He was making her pussy wet and her nipples hard, and making himself hard at the same time.

"Go ahead, Baby. I'm bout to get out your way."

"Finish playing your game, Baby. Everything will be ready in a minute," Cimone replied.

"Daddy," Ja'mone called out.

"Yes, sweetie."

"Can I play your game?"

"I don't care, sweetheart."

"Yesss!" she screamed with joy.

"Daddy, how she get to play?" Darius asked.

"You can play too."

He turned to Ta'darius and said, "I'm guessing you want to play too."

"Nah, I'm good, Daddy. I'm bout to go get on Facebook before I go to sleep. I gotta tell my lil baby good night."

"Boy you gon' be just like me," Jaquel said proudly.

"Why you say that, Daddy?" Ta'darius inquired.

"I see you like females a lot. How many you got now?"

"I got about four, but it's only one I really like."

"I suggest you stick with the one you really like because the other three might mean you no good."

"Alright, Daddy. I'm gon' see what you know," Ta'darius said in a joking tone.

"Listen to me, son. I'm telling you."

Cimone leaned out of the kitchen. "The food's ready everybody," she announced.

They all ran to the kitchen table to say their grace as a family and then dug in.

"The first one finished need to go take a bath and get ready for school in the morning," Jaquel said.

When everyone finished, Cimone retreated to their bedroom and Jaquel cleaned the table so they could all go bathe. Then he walked into the master bedroom and locked the door behind him. He started taking off all of his clothes and jewelry. As soon as he got relaxed, Cimone came out of the bathroom from showering. She was butt naked wrapped in a towel, and his dick instantly rose at the sight of her.

"You tired already, Daddy?"

"Hell nah! I was waiting on you mama."

Cimone slid the towel off of her perfectly shaped frame, and pushed Jaquel onto the bed on his back. She grabbed his thick dick and started licking around his head, pulling it in and out of her tiny mouth.

"Mmmmm... Daddy, I missed this dick," she said sounding excited.

"Get that dick, Baby," he said.

And that she did...she went so far down on his dick that she nearly choked, but she quickly regained control when she slowly slid it out and started sucking his balls. She didn't know what that did to a man, but she knew that he liked it from the way he pulled her hair.

"Damn, Baby...you got me hooked," Jaquel said.

"That's good, Baby. I would hate for someone to luck up on you," she said before she stuck his dick back in her mouth.

Slurp, slurp, slurp, slurp... "Your dick yummy, Baby," she said as she jacked him off while he skeeted in her mouth. She didn't miss a drop.

He was going limp, but Cimone got the jumper cables on his dick and brought it back up. Jaquel found some energy to bend her over and suck on her pussy. He was pretty decent in both areas, but he was a master at getting her pussy to cum. He fucked her with his tongue while inserting two fingers in her. She started fucking his fingers. Then he took his fingers out of her and started sucking on them. She kneeled there shaking her ass ready for some attention. That's when he spread her ass cheeks and licked all around the rim of her ass hole. She moaned with satisfaction, saying his name barely above a whisper. He flipped her over on her back and buried his face in her sweet juices. He softly grabbed her clit with his lips and slid his soft lips up and down it. She started going crazy, grabbing his head and moaning uncontrollably. She had came like two or three times already, but he wanted her to tap out before he fucked the shit out of her.

"Noooooo, Daddy. That's enough. I want that dick."

He lifted up and pulled on his dick to get it rock hard, then stuck it in her tight wet pussy.

"Oooh, Daddy! You feel so fucking good!" Alina screamed.

He pushed in and out of her warm wet pussy, catching a fast paced rhythm. She was loving every bit of her baby daddy. This was one of the many reasons they were still together. He grabbed her shoulders from underneath her arms and started plunging in her as hard as he could.

"Ugh, ugh, ugh, ugh, ugh, oooh! Jaquel, I love you, Daddy."

He didn't even respond. He started going even faster and harder. She screamed at the top of her lungs and they both came at the same time. Cum was dripping down their inner thighs. He just laid on top of her exhausted.

"I love you too, Mama," he said as he kissed Cimone.

They both smiled and enjoyed each other for the rest of the night.

***

Alina drove down the street feeling like a new woman. Having her own business made her feel like she was on top of the world. She picked up the phone and said, "I'm outside. Open the door."

The front door to where she was parked at opened and Chris was standing there naked as hell - dick hanging without a stitch of clothing on.

"I see you aren't wasting any time," she said.

"I mean, why should I? Look at you…and plus we never finished our episode," he said while ushering her into his kingdom.

"Wow, you have a big place."

"I also have a big dick," he reminded her as he pulled her close to him and started tongue kissing her.

She wore a long t-shirt with no panties on with some Sponge Bob slippers. He reached under her shirt and palmed her pussy, while inserting his fingers into her hot box. Then he looked into her eyes, grabbed the back of her neck, and guided her upstairs to a room full of sex toys.

"Damn. You a freak, Boy!"

He led her to a bed where a pair of handcuffs hung from each side of the headboard. She laid down in submission as he locked both of her wrists, to where she couldn't do anything but wiggle and squirm. He spread her legs, parted her pussy lips, and blew on her pussy. It tickled so she laughed very seductively. He went and got some caramel chocolate syrup, and began to dip each and every one of her toes into the syrup. She wiggled her toes from the chill of the syrup, but he slowly warmed them up using his mouth to suck every drop of syrup off of her toes. He inched his way up her legs and started licking her inner thighs. Alina was twisting and swaying her hips eagerly anticipating the feeling of his soft wet tongue on her pussy. He gave it a few licks just to tease and proceeded upward kissing her stomach before he made his way to her rock hard nipples. He began caressing them gently with his tongue as he continued upward and started licking inside of her ear. He backtracked to her neck and kissed and sucked it passionately like a vampire.

By this time, Alina's pussy was soaking wet and he could feel it on the tip of his fingers. His whole point was to get her so excited to the point she was willing to beg for him. He teased a little more, tracing his tongue around the outside of her pussy while fingering her ass hole. Just when he had her going crazy wanting him, he began sucking her clit. She was so turned on she started fucking his mouth like it was his dick. Chris was so determined to make his point that continued to suck her pussy even after she came in his mouth several times. He enjoyed watching her love faces as her pleased her; but now that she was ripe, he took the games to another level. He grabbed a 12-inch dildo and played with her ass hole, using some of the cum dripping from her as lubrication. After pressing the tip in gently a few times to loosen it up, he started pushing it in and out of her with light strokes. When he finished giving her pleasure in ways that she hadn't before imagined, Chris kneeled over Alina and made her open her mouth up wide. He began sliding his big thick dick into her mouth. It felt so good to him that he started fucking her mouth uncontrollably. She enjoyed showing her appreciation to him for the fine job he did pleasing her, so she wasn't the least bit bothered when her pushed that 12-inch dick of his all the way to the back of her throat. She was sucking and gagging simultaneously. He busted a vicious load in her mouth. Cum spilled out and was running down her cheeks. He wanted more! He un-cuffed her, bent her over, and began forcing his rock hard dick into her ass little by little. Her faced was pressed into the sheets, and she laid there moaning with satisfaction as he began taking full strokes deep inside of her. They were so into each other that they kept fucking and sucking all night - going at it like two pit bulls!

After it was all over, morning peeked through the window and Alina rolled over and said, "You pretty decent."

"You're not a bad catch yourself," Chris said. "The things you did with my dick had me going crazy!"

"Don't give me all the credit. You can drive a bitch insane with all the freaky games you like to play."

They both laughed and engaged in conversation.

"So what you up to these days? I know you still don't work with crazy cat."

"No, I own that beauty salon that just opened down the street from your job. I could never work with her ass anymore," Alina said.

"I been hearing about that spot. It's called Catching Hair, right?"

"Yep, that's it," she said as she got up and starting getting dressed. "It's about time for me to bounce. I have to go home and get ready for work."

"Is you coming back tonight?"

"Ummm... I don't know yet. I might be busy because today is Sunday. I have to go collect booth money and push some of these customers out. This is one of our busiest days," she said as she started making her way to the door.

"Aight, don't make me come up there in put you in a private room," Chris said.

They both started laughing, but Alina could tell from his comment that she had him exactly where she wanted him. She accomplished fucking him, but now it was time to fuck his pockets.

"I'm not about to be like that dumb ass bitch Skyy, and pay for some dick. He bout to pay for my services, and all my bills," she thought to herself.

"Well alright, Chris...just text or call me if you need me."

Her phone started ringing and she picked up to hear the voice of Monica on the other end singing

"You should've known better..." She glanced at her phone and saw it was Chris. When she looked up, he had his mouth open ready for some more action. Although she was tempted, she just smiled and walked out the door.

***

Everyone was at the shop except for Alina.

"Anyone seen Boss Lady?" Horace asked.

"She probably somewhere doing the nasty," Shuntae said. "I know she gone come in and say something bout her booth money."

"Probably! That girl fucking the shit out of somebody child right now with her innocent-until-proven-guilty looking ass," Fruity joked.

"Fruity, you dumb as hell," Kira said while laughing her ass off.

Ms. Janet walked into the shop with her hair looking a mess.

"Damn! Where he at Ms. Janet? We bout to beat his ass," Shuntae said.

"Where who at, baby?"

"Bobby Brown," she said as everybody laughed. "Ms. Janet it look like you got into it with a tornado!"

"Child, I been stroking with the motion," she sung. "Where's my lil cutie pie hair dresser?"

Just then, Alina walked in the shop. Everyone greeted her on her way to her station.

"There she is right there. I spoke you up, Baby."

"Hey Ms. Janet. I see you came back," Alina said with a smile.

"Honey child, I done been through it with this hairdo. It just couldn't take no more."

"Don't worry about it. I'm a hook you up," Alina assured her.

"Well, Baby, don't do too much hooking. I only got 25 dollars."

"You alright, Ms. Janet. You know I got you."

"Ms. Janet, you ever been to Henry's before?" Fruity asked out of nowhere.

"Child, I been up there before. I seen all them dicks and my blood pressure shot to the roof. I damn near had a sugar attack cause I was ready to taste everything in there."

"Owwee, Ms. Janet," Kira said.

They all laughed.

"Honey, I was at that other shop, and them folks ain't no fun like y'all." Ms. Janet said referring to Elite. "All they want to do is be up in a bitch lane. Shoot... They need to worry about their own issues," she said ready to give up all the gossip goods. "I overheard a real messy conversation they were having in there one day. The girl Skyy done asked to use the sissy bitch Nicky's phone, and Girrrrrrl... How bout she saw a picture of her boyfriend E-Way in there!"

"Get the fuck out of here," Alina said with a devious grin on her face because she had already suspected a little indiscretion between E-Way and Nicky.

"Yeah, Girl, she asked him why was E-Way picture in his phone. He told the dumb bitch he was about to file a missing person report," she said as she tooted her lips up in disbelief. "Girl, I couldn't do shit but laugh cause I caught a glimpse of the picture; and judging by that, it's obvious the punk and E-Way had some secret relations on the down low."

"Girl, I must have missed something. So...not only is some freaky shit going down on the low between this bitch man and her best friend, Nicky...did I hear something about E-way supposed to be missing?" Alina inquired further.

"Yeah, apparently E-Way ain't been coming home, and the shit got Skyy ready to send out a search party on his ass. He probably just somewhere with another one of his boyfriends," Ms. Janet said jokingly. "I doubt if it's all that serious. I ain't heard nothing on the news or anything."

"Well, damn! Ain't that about a bitch! Let me find out..." Fruity said as he tossed his hair out of his face. "I told you these niggas be out here on the low-low."

"Un-Un...all this so called friendship shit don't mean nothing! The same way you cross a mothafucka is the same way you'll get crossed back," Alina said while shaking her head. "I guess people have to learn the hard way that love don't love nobody..."

To be continued...

Exclusive Blueprint Publications

Search for already released titles on www.amazon.com.

Also, visit the official website at **www.exclusiveblueprintpublications.com**

https://www.facebook.com/ExclusiveBlueprintPublications/

https://www.facebook.com/groups/EBP.BookClub/

https://www.twitter.com/eb_publications

https://www.instagram.com/ebpublications/

For inquiries about literary submissions, social media, and general company information contact:

Exclusive Blueprint Publications

P.O.Box 68804

Indianapolis, IN 46268

Available Titles

A Gangsta's Demise

Upcoming Releases

- A Gangsta's Demise 2
- Love Don't Love Nobody_Part 2
- Drama King
- Loving Together, Loving To Get Her
- Breast Cancer